WHEN ELIZABETH AND HER COLLIE BECOME A CERTIFIED THERAPY DOG TEAM, THEY BRING COMFORT, SUPPORT AND LOVE TO MANY PEOPLE. But their work takes a deadly turn when they reach out to a small girl who holds the key to a grim murder as they uncover the shocking facts of a criminal conspiracy. Stalked by a shadowy menace, the little girl faces a terrifying threat to her life and the only one who can help her is the strange and wonderful collie named Kane. Only he can protect her as he confronts a grim kidnapper and a terrifying inferno in his struggle to fulfill his promise to keep her safe.

In FOREVER STAY, Kane's destiny was indelibly changed by a young boy and his family as his life and remarkable intelligence were placed in jeopardy. Now his adventures continue as he puts himself in harm's way and risks everything for the sake of those he loves.

GENTLE HERO is a suspenseful story for anyone who has known the unconditional courage and devotion of a dog.

GENTLE HERO

By Ace Mask

https://www.facebook.com/colliesofheathercircle

Cover Illustration by Cindy Alvarado

ISBN 13: 978-0-692-13064-3

ISBN: 0-692-13064-0

For
The Dogs and Handlers of Pet Prescription Team,
for the love and joy they share with others
through pet therapy

CHAPTER ONE

Officer Rob Martinez casually steered his police cruiser through the quiet streets of an industrial area located in a suburb of Los Angeles, driving his vehicle at a slow enough pace to observe the warehouses and manufacturing businesses housed there. Coldly illuminated in the darkness by glaring lights, many of the buildings sat securely behind heavily padlocked gates and chain link fences supporting strands of barbed wire to prevent trespassing. 1:30 AM didn't fall within his regular patrol schedule, but he had volunteered to cover for a friend who needed some time off. Martinez was young and unmarried and maintained a more flexible schedule than most, and he welcomed a shift that promised to be quiet and uneventful. Observing empty streets and parking lots he had been patrolling that night, he found everything calm and quiet.

Sipping a cup of coffee in the seat next to him, his partner Linda Anders was fighting boredom and drowsiness, having exhausted conversation topics that generally helped them pass the time. It would be another three hours before the two of them could clock out. She emitted a weary sigh and nodded her head from side to side to stretch the muscles in her neck.

As Martinez' attention turned from his perusal of the buildings along the route, he was startled to see, illuminated by his headlights, a small human figure less than five hundred feet before them. The individual was wandering down the middle of the street, headed straight toward the car. Braking, he strained to see who or what was approaching them.

"What?" Officer Anders asked as the car stopped.

"What's that?" Martinez responded, looking straight ahead.

Anders followed his gaze and squinted her eyes as she focused on the figure headed in their direction.

"What in the hell . . . ?" she muttered.

Though the small individual moved slowly, as if half asleep, it wasn't long before it was close enough for them to see that it was a young black girl, perhaps six years old. Her dark hair was combed into a single braid at the back, and she was dressed in pale pink corduroy overalls worn over a simple white shirt. On her feet, she wore sneakers, brightly decorated with Disney Princess characters. Her eyes were opened wide, and she stared directly into the officers' vehicle headlights with a look of combined confusion and terror.

The vision before him was so unexpected and out of place, almost dreamlike, that it took Rob a moment to understand what he was seeing before he could manage to move. Both officers stepped from the car and Martinez approached the child as Anders remained beside her car door.

The girl gave no indication she could see him as he knelt before her. Her wide-eyed expression remained fixed straight ahead, and she would have walked into him if he hadn't stopped her by gently placing his hands on her shoulders.

"Hey there," he said to her in a soft voice.

Although she stopped walking, she pulled her shoulders from his grasp with a slight moan.

"Looks like she's in shock," Anders deduced.

"Bring me that bottle of water from the front seat, will you?" he asked as he nodded in agreement. As Anders complied, he removed his jacket and placed it around the girl's shoulders.

"Can you tell me your name?" Martinez asked her. There was no response. "Your mom? Your dad? Are they around here someplace?"

"Here," Anders said, standing beside him and handing him a bottle of water.

"Any ideas?" he asked her. "Where's your maternal instincts?"

"No ideas," she replied. "Never had any relationship with kids outside of juvie."

Unscrewing the lid from the plastic bottle, he held the water before the girl's mouth.

"Here. Drink this," he said to her, but she remained unchanged.

He touched her lips with the water bottle and attempted to pour some into her mouth, but she turned her head slightly, allowing the liquid to dribble down the front of her shirt.

"I'll call for Child Services," Anders offered. "This is beyond us."

Sighing, Martinez stood, studying the girls face as he replaced the lid on the bottle.

"Well, I guess so," he said, looking around them for anyone to whom she might belong. "But let's get her out of this cold. Tell them we'll meet them at headquarters."

Anders nodded as she walked back to the car, contacting her dispatcher with the radio microphone mounted on her shoulder

"Will you come with us, sweetheart?" Martinez asked the girl as he lightly nudged her toward the vehicle with his hand on her back. Slowly, he managed to move her toward his car, but as he opened the rear door, she suddenly stopped, reluctant to step inside.

"It's okay," he said reassuringly. "You're safe with us. You're safe."

Though she offered slight resistance, he managed to lead her into the back of the car but instead of sitting on the seat, she huddled on the floor, wrapping her arms around her knees and burying her face. Martinez joined her in the back seat.

"You drive," he told Anders.

At Police Headquarters, Martinez found an empty room with a small sofa that he offered to the child, but she passed it up, preferring to sit on the floor in the corner. As in the car, she remained huddled there, her face hidden.

Anders elected to complete necessary reports and left the door ajar as she departed while Martinez seated himself on the floor near the girl.

The Officer had comforted survivors and many crime and accident victims in his seven years with the department, but this one perplexed and troubled him far more than any he had experienced. It may have been the child's age and innocence that touched him so deeply, but it was the mystery of the source of her shock and his inability to comfort her that affected him most. He had been giving a great deal of thought recently about the absence of a child in his life, and now he pondered what he would do if he were her father. What would he do to take away her suffering?

As he waited for the Child Services worker to arrive, he did his best to comfort her with soothing conversation.

"You're a very brave young lady," he told her. "I don't know what you've experienced, but I know it hasn't been easy for you and I wish I could be as brave. You know, maybe if you tell me a little about what happened, I could help you. Won't you give me that chance?"

None of his attempts to reach her yielded any change.

"Hey," he said as he tenderly touched her arm in an attempt to gain her attention. With a gasp, she pulled away, turning to her side.

"It would be best not to touch her," came a female voice from behind him.

Martinez turned to see a thin, middle-aged lady standing in the open doorway clutching several reports in her hand.

"I was just trying to find some way to get through to her," he explained as he rose to his feet.

The woman shook her head and indicated for him to come closer.

"We don't know what she's experienced," she spoke to him in a hushed voice. "She may have been sexually abused. The inclination is to want to hug them and comfort them, but physical trauma can sometimes make them even more upset. I'm Barbara Walker. I'm the caseworker."

Martinez shook her hand as she offered it.

"How do you get through to her?" he asked. "I think she's in shock,"

"Well," she said, nodding, "the first thing we'll do is get her to a hospital and get her checked out. I've seen cases that have taken days to get a response. Have you seen any sign of physical abuse?"

"No," he responded. "No bruises, no blood from what I can see."

"Hmm. We'll see if the doctors find anything."

"You may have trouble getting her to go with you."

"I'll try talking to her for a bit first, but help is on the way. I have a friend who's volunteered to help me get through on a couple of occasions. We've had pretty good luck with him. He should be here any minute."

"I'd like to know his secret for getting through," Martinez said.

"Oh," she replied with a slight smile, "it's no secret. When you meet him, you'll understand."

Turning from the officer, the caseworker approached the girl in the corner and knelt before her.

"Hello there," she said softly. "I'm Ms. Walker, and I'm here to help you. Won't you tell me your name?"

The girl did not move.

"Are you okay?" the caseworker continued. "Are you in any pain? Won't you tell me your name so I can help you?"

As she began to realize the hopelessness of her attempt to communicate with the child, there was movement in the doorway behind her.

A twenty-year-old woman stood before them, her right hand holding something behind her. Her hair was cut short, and she wore tan capris with a red shirt that appeared to serve as a uniform. On one side of the shirt was a logo that Martinez could not immediately read, but he could see the name "Elizabeth" embroidered on the opposite side.

"Are you ready for us?" the girl asked.

"Oh, yes," Walker said, standing. She turned to Martinez with a smile. "This should do it. Watch."

The girl was on the floor leaning against the wall, her face still buried between her knees. After a moment she could hear an unusual "click, click" sound on the linoleum floor as something approached her. With great force, she was able to avoid looking up. It wasn't until she became aware of a warm, panting breath on the side of her face that she felt her senses being pulled up to the light from the darkness in which they had dwelt. Turning her head slightly to look around the corner of her knee with one eye, she beheld a warm, friendly, comforting face.

She had never seen a collie dog before, but she looked him over as he stood next to her now. She studied his thick, flowing, sable coat, his long, pointed muzzle, ears erect but tipped slightly and held forward attentively, his head enshrined in a grand, white rough which surrounded his neck like a king's robe, his small brown eyes looking into hers with concern, and she knew she had never seen anything so beautiful. He wore a short, blue, canvas vest on which was embroidered several official looking certifications.

His tail wagged slowly from side to side, and he stood near her, his head tilted slightly to one side as if asking for permission to come closer. He didn't need to. The girl turned to him, placing her arms around his neck and buried her face in his luxurious coat as she erupted in sobs.

Holding his leash, Elizabeth spoke to the dog quietly.

"That'll do, Kane," she said.

CHAPTER TWO

Barely three months before his encounter with the frightened young girl at the police station, Kane strolled peacefully through the vineyards that surrounded the McLaughlin family home which was located in an inland valley near the Santa Barbara coast. Nearly a year had passed since the chaotic events occurred which had threatened to tear him from the family he loved and which had placed his life in peril. Now, on this bright, spring morning, he was tranquil and happy as he had been in his earlier days before his first master, an old man whom he loved and worshiped, had died, leaving him to his grandson.

The gently rolling hills on which the vineyards flourished were green and abundant with fruit that would eventually produce exquisite California wine. Thanks to a lease agreement with a nearby successful winemaker, a new irrigation system had recently been installed, making it possible for a healthy crop of grapes to thrive for the first time since a devastating drought had gripped the region.

Here and there, workers tended the fruit and cheerfully greeted the happy collie as he passed by. He would say hello to them as he did each day in his way, wagging his tail and pausing long enough to allow them to stroke his fur for a moment before he continued his walk, feeling blissful and contented. Occasionally he would encounter a rabbit or a deer which necessitated a loud "Woof!" and a speedy chase through the vineyards. He would continue his pursuit until the trespasser was sent scampering back into the nearby hills and only then would Kane stop, giving voice to a final warning bark which echoed after them as a caution. *"Return here at risk of life!"* it said.

This was his job in the vineyard, after all, he thought, but it was all bluff. Though the wildlife in the area took no chances, they came to realize he was indeed all bark and no bite and they would return each day to repeat the exercise.

After assuring himself that his vineyard (or so he thought of them) was free of pests, he redirected his attention to a more important responsibility, Ben. The boy, recently turned ten years old, was also wandering the vineyards somewhere nearby and a quick whiff of the breeze told Kane exactly where to find him. Running with a smooth, natural gait, his long, rough, golden fur rippled in the wind as the collie wound his way through the field to be by Ben's side.

Kane found his boy walking down a furrow between the planted vines. He held a broken branch of leaves and unripened grapes which he brushed against the vines as he strolled, repeatedly humming the refrain of a Beatles melody as he moved along. Sometimes the branch would brush against a worker as he passed but he was oblivious to the contact, and they either ignored his presence or called out a friendly greeting.

Joining him, Kane walked at the boy's side, occasionally sniffing a low-hanging branch as they passed. He knew Ben might walk like this for a long time, but he didn't mind. He was content to accompany him, and as he did so he found himself reflecting on the adventure he had experienced a year ago, and the unwanted attention that situation had invited.

He understood that Ben's late grandfather had only the best intentions when he implanted him with a microchip that dramatically increased his intelligence. The old man had hoped Kane would be uniquely qualified to help his grandson deal with his autism. But when it subjected the dog to experiments that threatened his life, a tug-of-war had ensued between Ben's family and a large pharmaceutical corporation over his legal ownership. Ultimately, the family reasoned that the only way to retain possession of Kane was to disable the implanted device, rendering it useless, and the corporation, bowing to immense public pressure, surrendered its claim of ownership.

Only Kane realized that the intelligence the device had generated did not regress after the microchip ceased to operate. He was determined to keep that fact to himself rather than bring chaos on the family again. It would be his secret alone.

Nearby, Sally parked her SUV in front of the two-story McLaughlin home which sat near the entryway to the vineyards. She mounted the steps to the front of the house, ringing the doorbell and calling out a greeting through the screen door. She had driven several miles to talk to her niece, May, face-to-face instead of talking to her by telephone. Their last conversation had been an emotional one and Sally wanted to be with her in case the news she was expecting to receive that day was upsetting. The lack of a prompt response from inside the house did not put her at ease.

A second "Hello" filtered through the screen eventually yielded a response.

"Come in, Aunt Sally," May called out to her in a voice far from cheerful. "I'm in the den." Sally could tell from the tone of her voice that the news was not good.

Sally found her niece in the den, seated in a comfortable, large armchair, facing out the open window that overlooked the grounds outside the house. She was sipping a liquid from a glass, an open bottle of whiskey on a small table beside her. Her eyes were wide and staring.

"That's probably not what you really need right now," Sally said, pointing to the bottle as she pulled up a chair beside her.

"Well," May said, pointing to a Bible lying on a desk nearby, "I'll get to that eventually, but right now I'll settle for this."

"Are you ready to tell me?" Sally asked.

May exhaled, set her glass down and rubbed her eyes with her fingers before finally speaking.

"Alveolar rhabdomyosarcoma," she said, carefully pronouncing every syllable. "That's what they said. Ever hear of it?"

"I believe so," Sally replied, wrinkling her brow, trying to recall precisely what the name described.

"Well, it's a childhood cancer," May explained. "They gave me a stack of reading material. It's on the kitchen table."

"We'll go through all of it together," Sally said softly.

"I thought it was just an insect bite. Just an insect bite on his calf. But it wouldn't go away."

May threw her head back and closed her eyes. "Why didn't I have him checked sooner?" she asked angrily.

"Now, don't start blaming yourself," Sally reprimanded. "That's not going to help anything. What are they going to do now? What's the next step?"

"Oh, there's the usual options, chemotherapy, radiation therapy. There's a clinical study going on in Los Angeles. Doctor Garfield recommends it. We would have to be there for a few weeks, maybe a few months."

"Then that's what you're going to do," Sally said, patting her hand. "I can look after the place here and in fact, I know just where you can stay. An old client of mine has a small house in Orange County that usually stays empty this time of year. He spends most of his time at his other home in Hawaii. He owes me for saving his Rottweiler a while back. I'll call him and set it up. You and Ben and Kane can stay there while . . . ."

"I refuse to believe this is happening," May suddenly exclaimed, leaping from her chair and beginning to pace. "It's not fair. After all Ben has gone through, and now *this*? He's only ten! I mean, it just can't be!"

"May," Sally tried to reassure her in a calm voice, "life isn't about 'fair.' In my sixty-nine years, I haven't seen a lot of that, but you're going to need strength, and faith and love to get you through this. Ben's going to need your full supply of all of those things."

Sally reached for the whiskey bottle and screwed the bottle cap tightly, then lifted May's glass and drained it in two large gulps.

"There'll be time for this later," Sally said, gesturing toward her with the empty glass. "Have you told Paul about Ben? How about Elizabeth?"

"Elizabeth's been in class. I'll call her in a little while. Paul was with us on a conference call when they told us the news this morning," May said with a shrug.

"This would be as good a time as any for him to resume the role of father. Will they let him come home?"

"He's supervising a pretty important job with that contractor in Afghanistan. There's no need for him to come home for this. Not yet. I told him to stay there. I mean, what can he do?"

"The main thing he can do is come home from that job and tend to his family," Sally admonished. "You're going to need some support."

"I'll be okay," May declared. She stood straight in an effort to appear strong. "I can handle this. With the right attitude, we'll lick this thing in no time and come right back home. He'll be okay."

The sound of the screen door slamming signaled Ben's return from the fields, and soon he stood in the doorway, his dog at his side.

"What did the doctor say about my bite?" Ben asked. "It's really bothering me today. It hurts!"

Inwardly resolving to allow Ben to see only strength and courage, she called her son to her side and did her best to be honest and open about his condition. He listened to her words, occasionally asking questions without becoming upset. It was as if he was being told about someone else's ill health, someone he didn't know. In the coming days, Ben would think on his mother's news as he tried to ascertain how it applied to him, but for now, his innocence allowed him to face what lay ahead without fear.

Kane was another matter. Though he did not wholly comprehend some of the words that were spoken, he made enough sense of them to understand that his boy's health was in danger and May's words, reassuring to Ben, were distressing to Kane. He could see through her façade.

CHAPTER THREE

When Kane later received his therapy dog certification, he had expected that he would be visiting young people in hospitals and seniors in assisted care facilities with an occasional session or two every couple of weeks with children's read-to-the-dog programs. He did not foresee the circumstances that would lead him to the side of a small, terrified little girl in the early hours of the morning inside a Los Angeles Police Station nor could he have known of the danger to which he and those he loved most would be exposed.

At first, his overwhelming concern was for Ben. Before the boy's grandfather died, he charged Kane with responsibility for Ben's safety, and it was an assignment the collie felt confident to assume. But Kane was powerless against this threat to his boy's health, and he was by turns confused, frustrated and depressed. He could only do his best to offer comfort to both Ben and his mother, and though he felt it wasn't enough, the magical healing humans derive from the company of a dog filled a prescription no medicine could provide.

Although another two months lay ahead before school would break for summer vacation, May was granted early leave from her teaching post so that she and Ben and Kane could temporarily relocate to Southern California.

The house Sally's client provided rent-free, with its three bedrooms and spacious backyard, worked out well for them. Though the nearly daily drive to the hospital in Los Angeles where Ben received treatment took almost an hour to navigate, the somewhat rural atmosphere of the Orange County neighborhood of Yorba Linda, with its scenic horse and hiking trails, was a welcome, comfortable, temporary residence for the little family.

Kane was not allowed in the hospital, so he spent many days alone and unhappy though he managed a cheerful reception for Ben who would often return home from his medical treatments drained and nauseous. Reacting to the often grueling combination of radiation treatments and medication, Ben had again become withdrawn as he had been before Kane had come to live with him, but he always managed to acknowledge the dog's kind greeting. The two would instantly snuggle close together on the front room couch as May covered her son with a soft blanket and he would promptly fall asleep. As they lay together, Kane wished for a way to absorb the misery Ben was experiencing

On a rare occasion when Ben was given a break from treatment, he and his mother were surprised with an unexpected visit from his sister, Elizabeth. On that particular day, his nausea was tolerable, and he cheerfully welcomed her and the gift she handed him. Hugging her mother, she joined him on the couch to watch him unwrap his present while acknowledging the gleeful wagging of Kane's tail by wishing him hello as she vigorously roughed the fur on his back.

May was pleased to see Ben react with joy as he unwrapped his gift to discover a 12 inch, battery operated, remotely controlled Godzilla figure. He promptly moved to the floor, and with a hand-held controller, he directed the toy monster to move toward Kane, giggling as the dog repeatedly barked at and dodged the object each time it came near.

While Elizabeth laughed at the antics of her brother and his dog, May stared at her daughter.

"How did you find time to get away from school?" she asked. "This is the middle of the week. Don't you have finals coming?"

"Not to worry," Elizabeth replied, now smiling at her nervously. "I'm here to help you."

Her mother's eyes widened.

"With Ben," Elizabeth continued. "I'm taking the rest of the semester off."

"In the first place," May began, anger rising in her voice, "I don't need any help. I'm managing just fine. In the second place, you can't just suddenly take off from college. How will you ever . . . ."

"Mom," Elizabeth interrupted, "I'm only twenty-one. I still have plenty of time, and Aunt Sally promised to refer me to a veterinarian down here where I can work part-time while Ben gets his treatments. Then I can go back to Davis again in the fall."

"Why didn't you think to consult me about this?" May asked as her voice grew louder. "We'll get through these treatments and everything will be fine. Let's not make this into a bigger deal than it is."

Elizabeth was mystified at first by her mother's annoyance before she realized she hadn't yet accepted the seriousness of Ben's condition.

"Well, I've taken leave now," Elizabeth said. "I can't go back until the fall semester. If you don't want my help and support, I'll do my best to stay out of your way, but let me at least be here with Ben while he gets through this."

With an angry exhale of breath, May threw her arms up in a gesture of surrender and stormed out of the room.

Turning her attention back to Ben, Elizabeth observed that he was repeatedly pushing the "forward" button on the remote control in his hand as the toy monster stalled against a wall, unable to advance while its legs continued to move in place in response to the boy's command.

Kane watched helplessly. He hoped Elizabeth's arrival would make a difference.

Soon after, Elizabeth struck upon an idea that would reward her in ways that she would never have dreamed possible, unaware it was also the beginning of a dangerous adventure.

CHAPTER FOUR

One day, while accompanying her mother and Ben to the Los Angeles hospital where he received periodic oncology treatments, Elizabeth set down the computer tablet. on which she had been passing the time reading a book. She yawned, stretched and surveyed the room about her.

The pediatric oncology infusion center was located in a spacious, open room festively decorated with colorful pictures created by young patients in crayon and watercolor which shared wall space with frolicking juvenile animal decals. Children varying in ages from toddler to teenager were seated in vinyl lounging chairs backed against the walls surrounding the room, and some of the younger children shared space with a mother or father, sitting in a lap or leaning into the breast of a parent seated next to them. Some of the children were being cared for by nurses and hospital staff who performed blood draws while others were connected to tubes which extended from their chest, stomach or arms to bags of clear liquids which hung from racks standing beside them. Additional tubes led to electronic monitoring equipment and computer terminals which displayed information about the treatments being administered. Here and there a child was distracted with a video game played on a computer tablet or smartphone, a few watched cartoons on television monitors mounted on walls nearby. Several dozed, the result of a sedative intended to help them tolerate the treatments they were enduring.

One corner of the room was designated as a crafts and recreation area and several children who were either in between treatments being given that day or who were siblings of those being treated were involved in coloring, pasting and scissoring, assisted by volunteers who patiently sat beside them. A couple engaged in board games.

Yet, despite every well-intentioned effort made to render the room friendly, cheerful, and fun, Elizabeth couldn't help but sense a slight gloominess that seemed to hover over the proceedings.

Until a door opened and a dog entered the room.

Seeming to smile, the female golden retriever, wearing a blue vest that identified her as a therapy dog and identified her as "Charli," sweetly wagged her tail as she looked about the room at the children. Eager to visit all, the dog was struggling with the question of which one to approach first. Her leather leash was held by a smiling lady in her mid-forties who wore jeans and a red polo shirt which displayed an embroidered logo near her left shoulder for a therapy dog organization that called itself Gentle Pets Therapy Team. Stitched on the opposite side was the name "Chris" and she wore a lanyard around her neck from which various pieces of official identification were hung.

As the lady and her dog entered, all faces in the room turned toward them, variously reflecting smiles, excitement, and curiosity. Avoiding those who were asleep and those avidly wrapped up in video games on their tablets, the therapy dog team approached an interested young man who cautiously extended a hand to stroke Charli's head as his mother, seated next to him, smiled her approval. While the dog enjoyed the physical attention, Chris engaged the boy and his mother in conversation which centered around Charli but also included stories about the patient's family dog as well. The visit was highlighted by a few tricks performed by the dog to the delight of all who observed and before moving on to the next patient, each was handed one of Charli's personal trading cards.

Elizabeth noted that as Charli and her handler moved about the room, most of the children who came in contact with the dog were at least momentarily cheered and distracted from the discomfort and emotional depression in which they had been consumed a moment before. Though she had seen for herself the effect an animal can have on human behavior and physical health, observing Charli as she administered her magic potion was, nevertheless, a revelation. When she noticed the interest Ben, seated next to her, directed toward the dog, she made an immediate decision.

"You know what?" she asked her mother, seated on the opposite side of Ben. "I'm going to get Kane certified as a therapy dog."

May looked up from the book she was reading.

"What?" she asked.

"I can't go back to school until the fall," Elizabeth reasoned, "the vet Sally referred me to has very little for me to do, I'm only annoying you by hanging around, Kane's sitting around the house worried sick about Ben, and this would be the perfect way for him and me to occupy our time!"

"Well. . . . ," May started.

"And," Elizabeth interrupted, "maybe then Kane could even go with Ben when he goes for all his treatments."

May could muster no valid disagreement with a decision that had already been made. It was typical of her daughter's determination and reminded her of the time a few years ago when Elizabeth decided she would study to become a veterinarian. Her resolution was immediate and irrevocable and, like now, she would brook no argument.

Jumping up from her chair, Elizabeth approached Chris and asked if she might talk to her when she had a moment. Chris cheerfully agreed and not long after was being peppered with questions about the procedures required for therapy dog certification.

Elizabeth learned that if her dog knew basic obedience and possessed the gentle temperament and aptitude for sociability with all animals and people of all kinds, she and Kane would likely be accepted for certification. For a reasonable fee, she and her dog would be required to complete eight one-hour classes over an eight-week period. Elizabeth excitedly took a business card which included a contact number for the organization.

"You know," Elizabeth thought, "this will probably be as therapeutic for Kane and me as it will be for the patients we visit."

Elizabeth felt a rush of excitement, but she didn't share with her mother one question Chris had asked her when told of Kane's background. It was not the kind of assignment she had imagined therapy dogs perform.

"How would you feel about visiting jails?" Chris asked.

CHAPTER FIVE

Within days of her first meeting with Chris and Charli, Elizabeth and Kane joined a handful of other dog teams at a nearby senior assisted care facility where they were to receive their instruction to become therapy dog volunteers.

The classes were conducted by the organization's director and trainer-at-large, a thin, lively, middle-aged lady named Claire Amory, whose high-energy level, friendliness, and lively sense of humor were buoyed by the seemingly bottomless paper cup of coffee that she invariably clutched in one hand. Her knowledge of dog behavior impressed not only Elizabeth but Kane as well, who recognized a kindred spirit in the energetic spark plug.

Though such things as how to approach an individual in a wheelchair or one using a walker or cane were taught in the class, the process mainly involved testing the dogs to see how well they behaved and reacted to many distractions. The training was primarily for the humans.

Early in the program, Elizabeth learned that the two most important characteristics required of a good therapy dog team are traits that cannot be taught.

For the dog, the most critical thing is temperament. Not every dog has a mild personality and an ability to get along with other dogs and humans of all types under all conditions. Although early socialization helps, a dog either instinctively possesses these traits, or he doesn't. Mellow temperament is not a teachable trait.

For the handler, Elizabeth discovered, the most important thing is common sense and the ability to read a dog's mood. A dog may have all the components needed to make a great therapy dog, but without the proper guidance at the other end of the leash, those talents may be wasted. Having a friendly, outgoing personality and the wisdom to know how to talk to people in varied, often stressful, troubled or gloomy situations is essential but one either possesses the qualities needed to be a good therapy dog handler or one doesn't, and common sense is critical.

At the start of the third training session, Claire was preparing the class for a meeting with a group of seniors living at the facility who volunteered to serve as experimental subjects for the therapy-dogs-in-training. While they waited in a nearby room to interact with the animal visitors and their handlers, the knowledgeable instructor was briefing her students as she paced back and forth in front of them. Suddenly she stopped in mid-sentence. Sensing a weird vibe, her eyes searched the room for a moment, seeking the source of the strange feeling before focusing her attention on Kane.

As she looked intently into his eyes, the collie was convinced that Claire was looking deep into his soul. It was as if she could see the secret he was so carefully hiding, and it scared him.

"This is the dog that was in all the news last year, isn't it?" she asked Elizabeth without taking her eyes from him.

"Yes, it is," Elizabeth responded. "But he's been deprogrammed, I guess you could say. No more super-dog intelligence, just a regular dog now."

As the trainer continued to lock her eyes on him, Kane nervously tried to think of some way to distract her. Turning to a neutered female Samoyed standing next to him, he began sniffing under her tail.

Elizabeth gave Kane's leash a gentle jerk to pull him away from the other dog as Claire watched him intently. Kane avoided her stare.

"Now what prompted that?" Elizabeth asked him. "You're normally the perfect gentleman."

"Stick around a bit when we're done here today," Claire said to her. "I'd like to talk to you."

The encounter continued to trouble Kane as he and Elizabeth visited the elderly residents of the facility. If, as he suspected, Claire did indeed see past his deception and could discern the true level of his intelligence, he worried that his life might once again become complicated. Added to his distress over Ben's health, Kane was consumed with worry, making his visit with the seniors difficult.

Nevertheless, he managed to spread cheer among them as they stroked his thick, soft fur and wondered why collies no longer enjoy the popularity they once knew. Many fondly reminisced over a dog they had known in their youth, and occasionally eyes would become moist with tears as the memory of a close canine friend long since departed was recalled. Elizabeth soon learned that often these were not tears of sorrow but rather tears of love shed over the peace and joy they experienced in a dog's company, and Kane, too, was comforted.

On this occasion, Claire felt the dogs and handlers were ready to meet another challenge in the training process and announced that the group would proceed to the third floor where residents who were experiencing the symptoms of dementia and Alzheimer's disease resided. Preparing her students for the behavior of the people they were about to meet, Claire described how the disease manifested itself and reminded everyone of the need to be consistently attentive to their dogs' safety. Though instances of the patients attempting to harm the animals were rare, Claire told them, they should nevertheless remain alert to the possibility and be prepared to pull their dogs back and move away from an individual if the need should arise.

"And here's something else you should keep in mind," Claire added. "Many of these people receive few, if any, visitors, and those that do come to see them never come often enough."

Confirming that all of the handlers were ready, Claire led the group up the elevator to the third floor where she worked the combination to the locked door which led to the Alzheimer's unit.

Passing through the entry, she led the group down a hallway to a recreation room where about thirty male and female residents were variously seated at tables placed throughout the area or on sofas and armchairs which lined the walls. Among the group were some seniors who seemed only minimally afflicted with Alzheimer's, while others appeared to be in far more advanced stages. Some watched a giant television screen mounted on a wall, seemingly unable to comprehend what they were seeing. Others drank fruit juice from paper cups which were distributed by white-uniformed caretakers.

As the therapy dog teams entered the room, several of the seniors verbally expressed delight but a few didn't seem even to notice the newcomers. Kane's olfactory nerve was immediately flooded with the odor of disinfectant, but his consciousness was filled with compassion. Though he did not grasp what afflicted these people, he was driven by a compulsion to be near them and something within told him that by doing so he could somehow help them. There were so many, he thought, so many that needed him.

Looking about the room, trying to decide which senior to approach first, Elizabeth spotted a spindly lady with long, straight, gray hair, seated alone at a small table next to a wall far removed from the other residents. Her face was set in a fierce frown as she stared, unblinking and unmoving, at her hands which were clutched into tight fists upon the table before her.

Sensing this was someone who might direct her anger at anyone who might attempt a visit, Elizabeth nudged Kane toward a smiling, bald gentleman who was waving her over to the armchair where he sat. The man lightly patted Kane's back while he repeatedly asked the same three questions: "What kind of dog is this? Is it a male or female? How old is it?"

After patiently repeating the same answers to the same questions four or five times, she became aware that Kane was pulling at his leash. He was attempting to lead her toward the frowning lady she had just passed. Though the lady remained as before, rigid and grimly looking at her fist upon the table before her, now she had extended one arm stiffly out to her side, palm open, apparently commanding Elizabeth to bring Kane near so that she might pet him.

Steeling herself, she allowed Kane to lead her over to the woman, prepared to pull him from harm's way if the need should suddenly arise.

When Kane stationed himself by her side, the woman, still focused on her fist, her demeanor unchanged, began to vigorously, almost violently, stroke the fur on Kane's back with her stiff, outstretched hand. Elizabeth watched apprehensively, waiting for a cue from the dog that he had endured enough of this harsh treatment, but he cast a look up at her that seemed to say, "*I'm okay. Let her work this out. I'm all right.*"

Indeed, as the woman repeatedly ran her hand along Kane's back, the strength with which she stroked him very gradually softened over time. While Elizabeth watched, the woman's entire disposition very slowly mellowed. The seemingly angry strokes became gentler, her clenched fist on the table slackened and then opened, the severe expression on her brow melted away, and though her unblinking gaze remained fixed before her, Elizabeth saw her entire body relax. Almost imperceptibly, a sweet, soft, smile formed on her lips. Kane very slowly wagged his tail from side to side.

Observing the peaceful manner that now enveloped the individual petting her dog, Elizabeth began to wonder: Where, in her head, was this woman now? Was she experiencing memories of a happier time? Wherever her mind had traveled, for this moment at least, she was completely and utterly at peace.

Elizabeth and Kane remained in the woman's presence until Claire moved toward the door and signaled to the group that it was time to move on. Quietly, Elizabeth told Kane that they must leave and as she led him away, she assured the woman that they would return to visit her very soon.

Claire held the door as Elizabeth and Kane, the last among the group, proceeded to exit. Before leaving, Kane stopped and turned to take a last look at the woman they had just visited.

The hand that had petted Kane now hung, motionless at her side, and though she was now visibly at peace, her gaze remained fixed, as always, on the table before her. The same soft smile lingered.

Kane and Elizabeth returned to the facility many times after that, but they never saw the woman again. That sweet smile he saw that day lingered forever in Kane's heart.

Later, as the other handlers were leaving the building, Claire motioned for Elizabeth to join her at a table on the patio located outside the facility. Kane accompanied Elizabeth with trepidation.

"Listen," Claire said to her confidentially, "I'm extremely impressed with the way you and your dog have progressed. Quite simply, you get it. If I were to give you your final certification test today, I have no doubt you would pass with flying colors. I have a desperate need for qualified therapy dog teams in several kinds of unique programs we've committed to, and I just don't have the right people to assign to them right now. These tasks are not for everybody because they require handlers and dogs with special sensitivity and good sense. I'd like to start assigning you and Kane to these programs. How would you feel about that?"

Kane was so relieved that this was the topic of conversation rather than any suspicions Claire might have had about him, he wagged his tail enthusiastically.

"Well, it looks like *he's* ready," Elizabeth said, laughing. "What kind of assignments are you talking about?"

"The first is a children's advocacy center," Claire told her. "It's a special location where kids, usually between the ages of four and fourteen who have suffered abuse, physical or sexual, or may have witnessed an act of violence, are brought to submit to a forensic interview with a trained therapist. The interview is observed by detectives, attorneys, children's advocates, whoever might have interest in the case, so they can determine if there's enough evidence to bring charges. You and Kane will be interacting with the kids before the interview to get them to relax so that they're more willing to open up to the interviewer. Now, in some instances, you and Kane may be required to be present in the room during the interview if the child insists on it. You might even be asked to accompany the child to court if the prosecution thinks it will help. Do you think you'd be up for that?"

"I ... Well, sure," Elizabeth stammered, nearly speechless. "I mean, this isn't at all what I expected. I thought we'd just be visiting kids in hospitals and libraries and meeting seniors in places like this. I never expected . . . ."

"Our group accepts some pretty unique assignments that some of the other organizations aren't willing to take on," Claire said, nodding. "It's not always easy as you might imagine and it takes a special team to deal with some of the situations that might come up. Most of the time it's not a problem, but it can sometimes become uncomfortable or emotional."

"Well, yeah," Elizabeth said. "I'm willing to do that, but don't forget, I'm going back to school in the fall and Kane and I still need time to spend with Ben. He's kind of the main reason we started this training."

"You'll pretty much have all the time you need," Claire assured her. "You can pick and choose your assignments, so you can schedule them to suit your needs."

Claire took a sip of coffee. "There's one other opportunity I'd like to offer you."

"Okay," Elizabeth responded, noting the importance in Claire's voice.

"We've been in demand by the Los Angeles Sheriff's Department for several new therapy dog programs they've implemented," Claire continued, "including several juvenile detention centers. Our participation in those programs has been very successful. The program I want to offer to you is a weekly visit to the Men's Correctional Facility and the Twin Towers Correctional Facility."

"Jails?" Elizabeth asked with some surprise in her voice. She remembered her conversation with Chris, but she hadn't given this part of the program much thought.

"That's right. They're about the largest in the United States. We only have a couple of teams handling these visits right now, but we need more. You'd be escorted by a Corrections Officer, and you'll be visiting many different kinds of inmates, some who've committed minor crimes, some much more serious, many with psychological issues, some of them even in chains."

"They reward the prisoners with therapy dog visits?" Elizabeth questioned.

"It's not exactly considered a reward. They've found that after our visits the inmates are often easier for the deputies to handle. Fewer problems. It definitely has an effect. But this kind of volunteer work isn't for everybody. We only have a select few teams willing and qualified to . . . ."

"No, no," Elizabeth interrupted. "I'm up for it. And I'm curious."

Claire said she would call her to set up appointments for briefings and background checks that would be required for both locations and assured her she would find the visits personally rewarding and compelling.

The visits would prove to be far more than that.

CHAPTER SIX

Officer Rob Martinez stood near the door of the interview room where the child he and his partner picked up earlier that morning sat as she hugged the collie named Kane. The therapy dog's handler sat nearby while Barbara Walker, the caseworker, pulled up a plastic chair next to the girl and began quietly questioning her. Though the girl had not yet started to speak, she had at least stopped crying, and the comfort she seemed to find being in the company of the dog convinced the officer that she would likely open up soon.

"This is Kane," Barbara told the girl. "I think he likes you very much."

As if to confirm that statement, Kane wagged his tail and touched his nose to the girl's cheek, which made her smile.

"Won't you tell Kane your name?" Barbara asked.

After a considerable pause, the girl finally responded. "Becky," she said very quietly.

"What's your last name, dear?" the caseworker asked.

The girl answered in a voice so meek, her response could not be heard.

Officer Martinez breathed a bit easier, knowing that now that the girl was relaxing a bit more, additional answers, including her last name, would be forthcoming. He decided to check on the progress his partner was making on the incident report.

Half an hour later, he was seated on Officer Anders' desk, located in the communal office space she shared with several other officers, nursing a cup of coffee as he skimmed through her report while she double-checked online lists of missing children.

Through a glass partition that separated the office from the hallway outside, Anders saw the young therapy dog handler and her dog as they passed.

"There goes Lassie," the officer said to her partner. "Mission accomplished, I guess."

Tossing the report down on the desk, Martinez suddenly stood and rushed to the doorway.

"Elizabeth?" he called after her, remembering the name embroidered on her shirt.

Surprised, she and Kane stopped and turned to face him as he approached.

"Oh," she said. "Hello."

"I was one of the cops that found the little girl this morning," he said, extending a hand for her to shake. "Officer Rob Martinez. Call me Rob. How'd you make out?"

Kane studied the man's face and attitude. He could instinctively determine a human's character within moments. It was a hereditary trait he shared with many animals, and he very quickly decided this guy was OK.

"I think we did well," Elizabeth said. "The lady from Child Services seemed pleased, but she's giving Becky a rest before asking more questions. I think they're taking her over to the hospital to be checked out."

"Your dog is incredible," he said, kneeling down and stroking the fur on Kane's neck.

"I don't have any experience in this kind of stuff of course, but it seems odd," Elizabeth mused with a frown. "I wonder what she saw."

"Yeah," he replied as he petted the dog. "I wish I knew."

A sergeant, holding Anders' report in his hand, leaned through the doorway.

"Officer Martinez! A moment?" He said, nodding back to the office behind him.

"Yes, sir," the officer promptly responded as he rose to his feet. He started to walk away before stopping and calling back to Elizabeth.

"Can you stick around for a few minutes?" he asked.

"Sure," Elizabeth replied.

Watching through the glass partition, she observed Rob as he and his partner appeared to be receiving orders from their sergeant. Had he asked her to remain because he wanted to discuss the case, or was he leading up to something else? Kane was sure any further discussion would only be the prelude to a social request. He didn't need any canine instinct to surmise that.

During the discussion, Rob had apparently referred to Elizabeth, because she saw them all glance in her direction at the same time after which the sergeant nodded. The meeting finished, the sergeant left the room as the two officers grabbed their hats and joined Elizabeth in the hall.

"You got any place to be?" Rob asked as they approached her.

"Uh, not really," she replied. It was still early morning and Ben and her mother would be asleep.

"We've gotta retrace our steps back where we picked up the girl a while ago, see if we can spot any evidence of any kind in the area," he said. "You and your dog care to go for a ride-along? I'd like to learn more about this therapy dog work you do."

"I'm Officer Anders," his partner said as she offered her hand to Elizabeth, a sarcastic smile on her face. "Officer Martinez here may even get around to asking you about that, eventually."

Rob blushed and smiled with embarrassment and Elizabeth took note of his awkward reaction. His sensitivity impressed her.

Though he wasn't familiar with the term, "ride-along," Kane guessed they were going on some kind of hunt, and he was eager to participate.

Behind the wheel of the patrol car, Officer Anders slowly approached the area where the frightened girl had been found. The morning sun had not yet appeared and, this being a Sunday, there was no traffic in the streets around the industrialized area.

Rob, riding shotgun, was listening to Elizabeth, who sat in the back with Kane, explain the therapy dog program through the metal grill that separated the front and back seats. Kane was staring out the window. He hadn't quite figured out the purpose for their trip, but as the car slowed, he detected an aroma he recognized and began quietly whining.

"What's up, boy?" Elizabeth asked, turning her attention away from Rob.

Kane whined a little louder.

"This looks like the spot," Anders said as she stopped the vehicle. She manipulated the car's spotlight to scan the area.

"Let's take a look around," Rob said. He and Anders grabbed their flashlights and exited the vehicle. "Shouldn't be long," he assured Elizabeth.

The front doors were left open as the two deputies searched the area. Kane nervously squirmed. The smell he picked up told him there was something important nearby. He needed to show them. Growing impatient with the two officers, he cast a quick glance at Elizabeth before frantically clawing at the window on his side of the car. Elizabeth knew him well enough to recognize that he was trying to convey something important. Leaning over him she unlatched the door, and as it swung open, Kane swiftly leaped to the street.

Elizabeth watched him as he began sniffing the road in a zig-zag pattern before following him.

"Uh-oh," Officer Anders said when she noticed Kane. "Lassie's on the job. She'll sniff out some leads in no time."

"He's a male," Rob informed her.

"And he hates being called 'Lassie,' Elizabeth joined in. "Don't underestimate him, either."

"A male, huh?" Anders commented. "I didn't know collies came in that flavor. Looks like he's on the trail of a female. Hot on the trail."

At that moment, Kane stopped in the exact spot where the girl had been enticed to enter the police vehicle. The scent was most active there. Lifting his head, he stared intently in the direction from which the girl had been traveling. The path led that way, he knew, and there was something significant out there. The scent was fading, but it was still strong enough to follow, and he knew he must trace it quickly while a light breeze carried the smell toward him. Ducking his head low to track the scent, he rushed down the street.

"Yep," Anders chuckled. "Gotta be a female."

"Come on," Rob said as he rushed back to the car. "We got nothing to lose. You drive."

Anders nodded as she and Elizabeth returned to the car.

Kane was moving down the middle of the street at a brisk walk as the police cruiser caught up with him and followed close behind. After a distance of two blocks, he had to stop and step to the side of the road as a small truck rushed by from the opposite direction. Returning to the middle of the street, the dog took a moment to recapture the scent. Moving forward, he came to the intersection of another road which crossed his path. There he hesitated. The girl's scent told him she had passed this way, traveling from one side to the other before returning and heading in the route from which he had been tracking, but he was unable to determine from which area the scent originated. Troubled with uncertainty, he decided to follow the trail to his right, and he moved hurriedly, worried that of the two choices, this might not lead to that "important" spot he knew was centered somewhere nearby. Now the scent moved from the street to the sidewalk.

Officer Anders steered the car around the corner and followed Kane closely as he sped down the street which, after a distance of one block, dead-ended in another cross street, this one lined with apartments and businesses. On one corner sat a small 24-hour liquor store, whose lights illuminated Kane's face as he stood in front of its glass door.

As their car pulled up to the curb in front of the store, the three passengers exited while Kane paced quickly in front of the entrance. As they approached, he suddenly bolted and headed back down the sidewalk in the direction from which they had just traveled.

"What the hell?" Anders wondered as they watched Kane run away. "Tell you what. I'll go in here and ask a few questions. You guys go ahead and see where he's headed. You can swing back by and pick me up."

Rob nodded and headed back to the car, followed by Elizabeth.

"Hop in front," Rob told her. "I hope he knows what he's doing."

"He's a pretty safe bet," Elizabeth assured him as she slid into the front passenger's seat next to the officer. Shoving the car into gear, Rob pulled away from the curb and accelerated to catch up with Kane.

The collie was racing down the sidewalk at his top speed. No need to retrace the scent that had led him in this direction. He knew it would take him back across the intersection. He couldn't figure why the smell had gone in two directions, but now that he was following this course he was confident it would lead him to the important object his senses told him he needed to locate urgently. On the opposite side of the intersection, he once again picked up the scent.

Reaching a point nearly a block down the street, Kane came to a sudden stop. Before him, he observed a six-foot-tall metal box which was installed on the weed-covered parkway which ran between the road and the sidewalk. It appeared to encase electrical equipment, perhaps for the street lamps, and it was there that the scent stopped. On the ground nearby lay two unopened peanut butter candy packages and several coins. A single dollar bill was blowing away from the scene. As he stood, trying to figure out what had taken place there, Rob and

Elizabeth pulled up next to him. While Elizabeth watched Kane, Rob surveyed the surrounding area. He promptly located the object that must have lured Kane to this spot.

"Hold on!" the officer muttered to Elizabeth.

Though there were no street lamps installed at this particular spot, the scene before him was illuminated by the pale light of the morning sky as the sun prepared to make its first appearance of the day. With the help of his vehicle's headlights, he could see that they had reached the end of a cul-de-sac. There were no buildings in the area where chain-link fences lined the dead-end street, separating the sidewalk from dark, empty fields, recently graded in anticipation of some future construction project.

Next to the curb, directly opposite the large metal cabinet which had stopped Kane, sat a hefty, white SUV.

As he stepped from his car, Rob's hand instinctively touched the handle of the police weapon that hung at his side. It was an abandoned vehicle, he knew. Whoever left it in this spot didn't want it found quickly.

"Please stay by the car," he called back to Elizabeth, who had opened her door and now stood watching him.

Pulling his flashlight from his belt, he shined it on the SUV, and as he slowly approached it, he could see that the driver's window was open. Kane joined him, remaining near his side and matching his pace. The dog detected something that the officer could not and a soft whine formed in his throat.

Just a few paces short of reaching the vehicle, Rob paused as his flashlight illuminated a shattered window on the passenger's side. Proceeding even more slowly, he directed the beam down into the seat behind the steering wheel, and at the door, he stopped as if frozen, startled by what he found. Momentarily removing his hand from his weapon, he reached into the SUV. Even from where Elizabeth stood she knew that he must be searching for a pulse.

"Stay there!" Rob yelled back to her before activating a radio which hung on his shoulder. As he requested assistance and described to the dispatcher what he found slumped in the front seat of the vehicle, he suddenly stopped in mid-sentence.

"Wait a minute," he said with astonishment, his hand still depressing the transmission button on his radio. "I know this man."

Kane looked over his shoulder at Elizabeth before turning and walking slowly back toward her. He knew she needed him right now.

CHAPTER SEVEN

"I'd like to request your permission to be attached to the Burton case, sir," Rob said, addressing his captain.

The officer had slept little since finding the dead body of his friend the previous day. He couldn't walk away from this case without helping to solve it, and now he sat in his commander's office, pleading for the assignment.

The man in charge, Captain Steven Takimoto, frowned at the lapse in protocol exercised by the officer. Elegant and slender, he projected a sense of strength and discipline intended to serve as a physical ideal for the men who served under him, though few were capable. He rankled at Martinez' break in convention.

"Do I need to remind you, Officer Martinez," the captain said sternly, "there is a chain of command?"

Rob winced. He was afraid he had blown his request the moment he stepped into the office.

"Yes, sir," he replied with all the humility he could muster, "I apologize for letting my eagerness to be a part of this case cloud my better judgment. The victim, Burton, he's an ex-cop. We used to work together."

"You mean before he was terminated for drug abuse?" Takimoto asked.

"Yes, sir," Rob nodded. "Well, that is, I don't think they got the facts straight on that. I knew Burton. I knew him well, and I find it hard to believe . . . ."

"Yes, well," the captain interrupted, preparing to dismiss the officer, "an investigation into the matter came to a different conclusion."

A balding, plainclothes detective, whose mustache hid his mouth, and whose full stomach hid his belt buckle, stopped into the captain's doorway and leaned lazily against the doorframe.

"Got him!" he declared, making no acknowledgment of Martinez.

Takimoto smiled.

"No casualties? No mess?"

"Case closed," the detective replied with a smile. "Oughta make the mayor's folks happy."

"Well, Officer Martinez," the captain said, "there you have it. Case closed. Detective Mosher here just arrested Zach Burton's murderer."

Nodding to the detective, Takimoto explained. "The officer here was requesting to be assigned to the case. He and the victim are old friends, he tells me."

"Really?" Mosher said, looking at Rob, sizing him up. He finally walked into the office, seating himself in the chair beside him before finally speaking again.

"You remember why Burton's badge was taken away, don't you?" Mosher asked him.

"Yes," Rob began, "but I don't . . . ."

"And you know when we found his body yesterday, a package of heroin was in the seat right there next to his body," Mosher interrupted.

"Yes, I do," Rob responded. "In fact, I found the body and I found . . . I found the . . . the evidence."

"There you go," Mosher declared with an air of finality. "Good work, Officer. And now, just now, I arrested the gang member that murdered him in a botched drug deal. So it's over now. You can bury your friend just as soon as they finish with him in the morgue."

The detective started to rise from his seat.

"The little girl we found wandering . . . ," Rob began.

"She was Burton's daughter," Captain Takimoto confirmed.

"Right," Rob agreed.

"Thought you said Burton was your pal," Mosher asked with a hint of suspicion in his voice. "Why didn't you recognize his daughter?"

"I haven't seen him for years," Rob explained, "not since he left the force. She was just a baby then. What did she tell you?"

Mosher appeared to be growing impatient with the officer.

"Not a hell of a lot," he said. "We figure Burton must have let her out of the car someplace. Not sure. He must have planned on picking her up after he unloaded the merchandise, I don't know. Anyway, we're finished with this, officer."

"Yes, but. . . ," Rob began.

"The girl will be interviewed in a couple of days," Takimoto interrupted. "She's scheduled for a forensic interview over at the Children's Advocacy Center."

"Interview?" Mosher reacted with surprise. "What's the point of that? We got all we need to send the perp to the executioner."

"Until you interview the daughter," the captain advised him, "you don't have every single detail. The interview has been scheduled."

Mosher was visibly worried.

"I need to attend that interview," he said.

"Of course you do," Takimoto responded, preparing to dismiss his visitors.

"Sir," Rob stopped him. "May I attend that interview?"

"Oh, for the love of . . . ," Mosher snorted with impatience.

"Your interest in this case is finished," Captain Takimoto bristled. "I'm sorry for the loss of your friend. End of discussion. You are dismissed, Officer Martinez."

Realizing there was no further appeal, Rob stood, saluted his superior and exited the room, passing a young officer seated at a desk in front of the captain's office who seemed to take an unusual interest in him. Rob was halfway across the outer office when he heard Mosher call his name. He stopped amid the desks and staff stationed around the room and waited as the detective approached him.

"This isn't your case," Mosher said in a quiet but threatening voice as he leaned into him. "So just butt out and mind your own business, OK?"

Rob resented the unspoken threat Mosher's admonishment implied.

"Say," he said, suddenly remembering. "My partner tried to get video from the liquor store where Burton left his little girl. The manager told him he'd have it for her later. Did one of your investigators go back and pick it up? Did you find anything on it?"

"We're on it, okay?" Mosher said, glaring at him.

"How is his wife taking it?" Rob asked, undeterred.

"You mean his *ex*-wife?" Mosher asked with a sneer. "She threw him out of the house a couple years ago. Probably had it with his drug problem. Anyway, don't you worry about it."

"No worries here, Detective," Rob replied cheerfully.

As the two men talked, a short, balding, heavy-set man in his late thirties, dressed in an impeccably tailored suit briskly brushed by them on his way to the captain's office. Martinez and Mosher watched for a moment as the man marched into Captain Takimoto's office and eagerly shook his hand.

"That would be the mayor's number one man right there," Mosher said, "coming to congratulate the department on catching Burton's killer, no doubt."

Turning back to Martinez, the detective eyed his subordinate.

Rob placed his hat on and briskly tapped the edge of the brim in an informal salute.

"You have a good day, sir," he said with a smile as he turned and left the office.

Detective Mosher knew damn well the officer wasn't through asking questions. He would have to be watched.

As he made his way from the department, Rob was delighted to receive a phone call from Elizabeth, and he paused in an outer hallway.

"Ready for more excitement?" he asked.

"What?" she said, nervously. "Oh. No. I just wanted to . . . ask a favor of you."

"To protect and serve, that's our motto," he replied.

"I told you about Kane's past," Elizabeth continued. "He's been at the center of a lot of attention, and now we just want him and Ben to be able to lead a normal life like any other boy and his dog and, well, if the news media got ahold of his participation in last night's incident . . . ."

"Hero dog strikes again, huh?" he asked.

"Exactly," she said with relief. "I haven't even told my mother about it. Heavens, if she knew I was out investigating a murder case . . .

"I understand," he assured her. "Not a word. I promise. How's your brother doing today?"

"Right now, he's sitting on the couch with Kane watching television," she replied with a sigh. "It breaks my heart to see him like this, so down and sickly. He's been through so much."

"Tell you what," Rob said in an effort to cheer her, "I'll drop by later this week with my patrol car and take him for a ride. Let him blow the siren a bit. Maybe it'll lift his spirits a bit."

"Oh, I bet he'd love that," she replied.

There was an awkward silence before he spoke again.

"Well, okay then. I'll do what I can to keep Kane out of the papers and I'll . . . I'll see you in a couple of days."

Elizabeth thanked him for calling and disconnected. She sat smiling for a moment, amused at his apparent interest in her, and after a few moments her phone rang.

"Hi," said the voice on her phone. "It's Claire. Hey, are you and Kane available for an appointment on Thursday morning?"

After checking with her mom, Elizabeth confirmed she was available.

"Great," Claire said. "You know the little girl you met at the police station the other morning? They need you and Kane to be with her for her forensic interview at the Children's Advocacy Center. She specifically requested Kane."

CHAPTER EIGHT

On the morning Kane and Elizabeth arrived at the Children's Advocacy Center for their therapy dog appointment, they were overwhelmed by a sense of tranquility as they entered the serene, park-like setting on which the welcoming, two-story, home-like building was located. They soon found that the tranquility they sensed was prevalent throughout the center.

They were met at the door by a friendly young female volunteer named Mary, who welcomed them and thanked them for their service. Mary made a particular fuss over Kane, and he was comforted by her attention as she escorted them to one of the family waiting rooms. It evoked a child-friendly atmosphere with comfortable furniture and a large, inviting fireplace on whose mantel sat a bevy of teddy bears and other plush animals while shelves were stocked with toys and games. Kane was sure he would like this assignment.

Mary explained that the CAC was staffed with volunteers and paid professionals trained in child psychology and that the goal of the center was to provide a forensic assessment of child abuse allegations in an environment designed to reduce the trauma to child victims by minimizing the number of interviews for evidence collection. Rather than subject a child to questioning in a sometimes cold, unfriendly police interrogation room, the CAC provided law enforcement, prosecutors, child protection workers and relevant agencies a calming, helpful resource in which to gather information.

To empower and comfort young victims, therapy dogs were employed to greet the children and families who visit the facility. Though extremely rare, if a child was particularly resistant to relating a traumatic experience and if the interviewer deemed it appropriate, she was told, the dog might be required to accompany the child through the entire interview process. This was the task to which Kane was assigned.

Shortly after their arrival, the doorbell rang, and Mary opened the door to admit Becky and her mother. Kane recognized the little girl and noticed that she and her mother seemed very tense. The young mother wore an expression one might expect to see on a parent's face who was preparing herself to be told by a doctor that her child had a terminal illness with only a week to live.

As Kane stepped toward them, however, his head held low in a semblance of humility, ears flat against his skull, his tail wagging slightly, and when they beheld the warm, inviting, room and its comforting embellishments, their tension could be seen to melt away. If the mother had spoken, Elizabeth thought, she would have expected to hear her say, "*Aaah. This isn't what I expected at all. Everything will be OK now. Lassie's here.*"

Squealing with delight, Becky rushed to Kane and, kneeling before him, wrapped her arms around his neck.

Mary cheerfully greeted the visitors and introduced Pauline, Becky's mother, to Elizabeth, as she offered her a seat on one of the couches. Pauline was thin and slight with a creamy brown complexion contrasting with a warm, cheerful smile that made her immediately likable. Becky sat comfortably on the floor with Kane and was joined by Elizabeth while Mary provided her mother with paperwork to complete as well as packets of information regarding assistance programs available to help families through traumatic events. She explained to her that Becky would be interviewed by a trained child psychologist in a comfortable room upstairs. The meeting would be monitored via closed-circuit TV in a separate room by disciplinary teams associated with the case, including prosecutors, law enforcement investigators, and child protection social workers. A digital recording was to be made for future legal reference.

As Mary was explaining this to Pauline, another CAC volunteer passed through the room en route to the stairs which led from the playroom to the interview room on the upper floor. She paused before climbing the stairs to introduce three individuals that accompanied her which included Barbara Walker, a district attorney named Mike Rickenbacker and Detective Mosher.

As she introduced the detective, Kane could feel the muscles in Becky's body tighten as she held him even closer. She must have encountered this man previously he surmised, and she was not at all happy to meet him again. Kane looked the man directly in the eyes. He decided to keep a watchful eye on him.

After the group ascended the stairs, Mary excused herself for a moment and left the room.

"I can't thank you and your dog enough for supporting Becky through this," Pauline said to Elizabeth after Mary left.

"Oh, no thanks are needed," Elizabeth responded. "We're glad we could be of help, and Kane loves being with children."

At the sound of his name, Kane looked up at Pauline and wagged his tail.

The two ladies indulged in small talk while they awaited Mary's return. Elizabeth knew not to bring up the homicide or any details concerning the case and instead guided the conversation to unrelated matters.

"Does Becky have a dog?" Elizabeth asked

"No. Zach wanted to get Becky a puppy," she said as her eyes grew cloudy, "but after we separated, Becky and I moved into an apartment and I had to get a job, so I was gone all day and our landlord doesn't allow animals anyway ."

Mary returned, accompanied by a friendly woman in her mid-forties who was introduced as Karen Hampton, the therapist who would be conducting Becky's interview.

Karen greeted Pauline and Becky warmly. After engaging her in conversation regarding Kane, she explained to her that she would be accompanying Becky to a room upstairs where the two of them would talk. She assured her that she was not in any trouble and that she would be pleased if Becky would come with her.

The girl became very still and silent and placed her face next to Kane's neck.

"Would you like to go with me, Becky?" Karen asked when she didn't respond.

"Can Kane come with me?" Becky asked in a voice that could barely be heard.

"Well," Karen replied with a sigh, "he'll probably have to stay down here and wait for you, but he'll be here to greet you just as soon as we've finished talking."

There was a long silence before Becky responded.

"No," she finally said. "I want Kane to go with me."

A look of concern and uncertainty spread over Karen's face as she stood before the child and made several attempts to convince her to accompany her alone, but her pleas were useless.

"Would you mind coming with me a moment?" Karen asked Elizabeth.

"Of course," Elizabeth replied, then turning to Becky, she said, "Kane and I are going need to talk to Karen for just a moment. We'll be right back, OK?"

Reluctantly, Becky released her grip on Kane who followed the psychologist as she escorted them up the stairway.

Karen opened the door to a conference room where Barbara Walker and Rickenbaker sat waiting for the interview to begin. Mosher sat sullenly in a chair in the corner, nursing a cup of coffee.

"Problem," Karen began, addressing the group. "The witness is reluctant to join me in the interview room."

"That's not a problem," Mosher said in a dismissive tone. "We don't need her testimony. We've got all the information we need."

"She may give us some new information," Rickenbaker said with a frown. "I think we would be remiss if we didn't hear what she has to say. That is, if she can be persuaded to talk."

Mosher was preparing to disagree when Karen continued.

"Actually," she informed them, "she's likely to tell you everything she knows if we allow her to be accompanied by the therapy dog."

Mosher snorted sarcastically.

"Is that something you've done in the past?" Rickenbaker asked.

"Very rarely," Karen replied. "The therapy dog organization requires that the dog be on leash and accompanied by the dog's handler at all times, which means Elizabeth here would have to join us."

"Fine," Mosher scoffed. " Why not see if there's anybody in the woods would like to get in on this?"

"Elizabeth would be required to be completely disengaged," Karen said, ignoring the remark. "She would have to remain invisible, a part of the wallpaper, regardless of what takes place, even if the child acts out."

"Of course, Elizabeth's presence means the defense could require her to testify because she would be a witness to the interview," Rickenbaker considered.

"So's the dog," Mosher added cynically.

Rickenbaker was visibly annoyed at the detective's continued negativity.

"Let's try it," the Deputy D.A. decided.

"You think you can do this?" Karen asked Elizabeth.

"Absolutely," Elizabeth affirmed.

As Karen led her from the room, Mosher grumbled, "What a horse and doggy show this is turning out to be."

It didn't take long for Karen to convince Becky to join her for a "talk" when she was told that Kane could join them. She was escorted to a moderately sized room that was likely to have served as a children's bedroom at one time. Though she was timid at first, Kane walked next to her, and with her hand on his back for courage, she settled into a large, thickly stuffed armchair that was positioned to face the seat occupied by Karen. Elizabeth sat behind Becky, remaining as quiet and unobtrusive as she possibly could. A video camera mounted on a tripod was focused on Becky.

Karen began by asking the girl general questions about how her week had been going and inquiring about her likes and dislikes. The questions were answered in a soft voice. As the interview proceeded, Becky interrupted.

"I want Kane here in the chair beside me," she said.

"Let's make a deal," Karen said to her. "Kane can sit next to you if you promise to speak in a louder voice. Will you do that for me?"

Becky agreed, and Karen nodded her approval to Elizabeth. Kane needed no coaching to step up onto the chair beside the little girl as she moved aside to give him room. He found just enough space to lay down beside her.

"Now," Karen said in a soothing voice, "I'd like to ask you what happened on that night, the last time you saw your father. Are you OK with talking to me about that?"

Becky focused on the fingers of her hand as she slowly scratched the fur on Kane's back. After a moment, she nodded her head.

"Good," Karen said cheerfully. "Where were you and your father going that night?"

"We were supposed to go to Edwina's birthday party," Becky replied slowly. "That's where my daddy was taking me. We were supposed to go there but we couldn't because . . . ."

"That's alright," Karen reassured her. "Take your time. When your daddy picked you up, where did you go?"

Becky shrugged. "I don't know where we were," she replied.

"Did your daddy say anything?" Claire asked.

"He said we were going to Edwina's birthday party, but something was bothering him."

"What was bothering him? Do you know?"

Becky shrugged again.

"I don't know," she said. "He just kept looking in the mirror. I think somebody was following in a car behind us, and I think he was scared or something."

"Did he say anything about the car? Did he say anything about why he was scared?"

Becky shook her head slowly.

"I was getting scared too because he was scared," Becky replied. "So we played a game."

"Will you tell me about the game?" Claire asked.

CHAPTER NINE

"Lay down as flat as you can on the seat," Zach Burton said to Becky.

Even though she could tell he was trying to divert her attention from the vehicle he was watching in his rearview mirror, Becky agreed to play along, hoping the game would relieve her of the growing uneasisiness she was experiencing.

"Mother may I?" she called to him from the back seat.

"Yes you may," he replied with a false note of cheerfulness in his voice.

Lifting the shoulder strap of her seat belt over her head and placing it behind her neck, she was free to lay her body sideways. This enabled her to rest her head on the vehicle seat while the lower portion of her body remained in the booster seat, restrained by a lap belt. From that position she was able to see, in the rearview mirror, that a large, black SUV was following them. She could also see the reflection of her father's worried eyes.

"You have to be standing up to play Mother May I," she said to him. "You can't play it sitting down. How can you tell who wins?"

"Well," her father said distractedly, "we're trying a new way to play it. Just stay down there like you are. Pretend like you're invisible."

"Okay," she agreed with a sigh, "but it's a pretty dumb way to play the game."

Without signaling, he quickly turned a corner and accelerated. Missing the turn, the vehicle behind them skidded to a stop, backed up and took the turn, trying to catch up.

Becky's father continued this tactic, each time managing to place distance between himself and the SUV behind them.

"Daddy, I'm scared," Becky declared, on the verge of tears but still maintaining her position.

"No, don't be scared," he tried to reassure her. "It's okay. Daddy's just having fun with the guy behind us. He'll be gone in a minute. Just lay still for a minute, honey."

"This isn't fun, though," she whined.

"Okay, okay," he responded nervously, looking anxiously at the front of the closed offices and industrial buildings that lined the street they were traveling. A neon sign illuminated a liquor store on a corner one block ahead of them. Zach glanced back at his daughter.

"Here's what I need you to do," he said to her quickly, "and this is very important. Are you listening, sweetheart?"

"Uh huh," she responded meekly.

Her father dug his hand into the front pocket of his jeans and pulled out a five dollar bill. Reaching over the back of his seat, he tossed it to her.

"I'm going to stop real quick in front of this store up here," he said. "When I do, I want you to jump out of the car just as quickly as you can, and I want you to *run*, you understand? I want you to *run* inside the store as fast as you can and buy you and me some peanut butter cups. Can you do that for me?"

"Okay, but where will you be?" she asked.

"I'm going to just drive down the block a little ways," he told her, "and then I'm going to turn around and come back and pick you up out front, okay? You wait for me there."

"Okay," she agreed, "but hurry back."

"I'll be back just as quick as I can," her father assured her. "Now, are you ready?"

Becky was ready, but she was sure she didn't like this one bit. Even the candy was not enough enticement to change her mind, but she was willing to do whatever her father asked her to do. He looked over his shoulder at her response, and she silently nodded to him.

"Alright," he said, "here we go then. I'm going to turn this corner up here and make a sudden stop. Just as soon as I do, unfasten your seatbelt, jump out of the car and run into the store as fast as you can. Ready?"

Swallowing deeply, Becky verbally agreed as she grabbed the seatbelt release button, ready to make her move.

Confirming that the vehicle behind them was at a sufficient distance to miss the action he was about to undertake, her father skidded around the corner on which the liquor store was located and made an abrupt stop by the curb.

"Now!" he shouted to Becky who disengaged her seatbelt and reached for the door handle as her father simultaneously activated the dashboard button to unlock it.

Throwing open the door, she hopped from her seat to the sidewalk.

"Hurry back quick, Daddy!" she yelled as she slammed the door behind her and ran toward the store.

"I love you!" she heard him say as his car pulled away and raced down the street.

As she swung the door open and rushed inside, she was aware that the black SUV had turned the corner as it followed after her father's car. She hoped the driver hadn't noticed her run into the store and she stopped in the doorway a moment to watch it as it raced past. What she didn't see as she turned away, was a black sedan that also sped around the corner close behind. The driver of that vehicle saw the small figure that had just entered the store, and the car pulled to a stop.

Inside the dingy, poorly maintained liquor store a bearded man, half awake, sat behind the cashier's station nursing an energy drink while he watched the snowy image of a small television resting on a ledge behind the counter. The man paid little attention to Becky as she entered and he cast only a cursory glance at the screen of a security monitor that sat on a shelf behind him amid the cigarettes, as a short, balding male adult dressed in a light colored suit entered the store. The cashier judged the man, who stopped a couple of steps past the doorway as he glanced around the store, to be of no concern, due to his well-dressed appearance. Probably the little girl's father, the employee figured.

Looking through the candy displayed on racks in an aisle near the cashier, Becky located the peanut butter cups and secured two packages. Before turning to walk to the counter, she was startled to see the suited man who stood near the door, at the end of the aisle watching her. It was the fact that he only stood looking at her, without moving, without speaking, his eyes narrowed in an expression of suspicion that chilled her, and for a moment she froze, returning his stare in wide-eyed fear.

The sudden sound of a cell phone ring caused her to jump, and the man reached into his jacket pocket, grabbed his phone and held it to his ear, while his expression remained unchanged and his focus remained on Becky.

"Yeah?" he quietly said into the phone. After listening to the caller for a few seconds, he said in a quiet voice, "Stay there. I'm on my way."

Placing the phone back in his pocket, the man suddenly flashed an artificial smile at Becky. The smile terrified her, and she was preparing to rush past him into the street to look for her father when the man quickly turned, casting a brief glance at a surveillance camera mounted above the doorway as he exited the store and returned to his car.

Her heart pounding wildly, Becky rushed to the counter and laid down her candy, pushing her five dollar bill to the cashier. He reached for the money, barely glancing at it and the merchandise before ringing up the purchase. He absent-mindedly shoved the change across the counter without counting it or offering a receipt or a bag.

The chilly evening air felt good on her face as Becky rushed from the store and stopped on the sidewalk outside, looking down the street where she had last seen her father. Impatient and worried, she began walking in that direction. He had told her he wasn't going far, so she figured she could find him nearby.

As she neared the end of the block, she became increasingly dismayed and disturbed. There were only offices and small warehouse buildings along the way, all closed and empty, no one around she could ask for help. Reaching the cross street, she hesitated until she heard voices coming from someplace further down the road ahead of her. The voices were yelling, and they sounded threatening, but she was sure that one of them belonged to her father. Excited, she rushed crossed the street toward the sound.

She hadn't gone far before she saw that the road ended in a cul-de-sac. Her heart leaped when she saw her dad's car, parked at the end of the road. She would have called out to him but the large, black SUV was parked in front of her father's vehicle and behind him sat a dark sedan. Two men stood by the open window where her father was seated behind the steering wheel. One of them, a tall, thin, black man, stood with his hands in the pocket of a black leather jacket. The other man, who was now talking in a quiet but threatening voice, was a white man dressed in a suit.

Becky nearly screamed when she recognized him as the man in the liquor store.

Desperate, she turned back in the direction from which she had come, but all was dark. No traffic, no one she could call out to for help. She now knew her father had ordered her into the store so he could confront these people without her, so she knew better than to rush up to him now. Instead, she spied a large, six-foot metal box that was located on the parkway next to the sidewalk. Unseen, she rushed toward it. Hiding behind it, she watched the events unfold.

Eventually, the man in the suit threw his hands up in the air before walking back to his car. He opened the door of the sedan and slid inside. The other man pulled something from the pocket of his leather jacket as he stepped up to her father.

What followed left her speechless and in shock.

Becky had done her best to relate the details of that awful night to Karen when she was questioned about it a few days later at the Children's Advocacy Center, but she was unable to continue when she reached the point in her narrative in which her father was murdered.

At her side, Kane snuggled close and placed his muzzle on her lap. He didn't comprehend everything she had said, but he had grasped enough of it. What perplexed him most, was his inability to explain to himself why people behaved violently toward one another. He could understand the motivations of his fellow animals, but humans often seemed to act in ways he could not fathom, sometimes killing each other without reason.

Realizing that Becky was nearing the limit of her endurance, Karen decided to wrap up the interview.

"May I ask you just a couple more questions, Becky?" she asked.

The girl shifted in her seat and paused before nodding her head. Kane hoped the questions would end soon. He was distressed by the girl's discomfort.

"Can you describe what the two men looked like?" she was asked.

Becky shrugged.

"If I showed you some pictures," Karen persisted, "do you think you could pick out which men you saw?"

"I don't know," Becky said, shrugging again. "Maybe."

"There!" Rickenbaker said from the next room as he and the others watched the interview on a television screen. "*That's* why we needed this interview. There's an additional suspect involved."

"And you think she's going to be able to pick him out, assuming we even have a picture of him?" Mosher said, shifting in his seat.

"Pressure the suspect you have in custody," Rickenbacker suggested. "Get him to put a name to the suit. Get the video from the liquor store. You're an investigator, do your job, dammit!"

"Whatever you decide," Barbara Walker interrupted, rising from her chair, "I'm pulling the girl out of this interview. That's enough for one day."

"Agreed," Rickenbaker nodded.

"I hope you find your second man," Walker said to the detective. "Until you do, this little girl's life could be in peril."

CHAPTER TEN

Elizabeth was getting dressed a few days later, as she prepared to attend the funeral service for Zach Burton, while Ben sat listlessly on the sofa in the front room of the little house the family had been loaned. Staring blankly at a cartoon program on TV, he held his Godzilla toy in one hand while his other hand rested on Kane, who lay beside him. His mother sat before her laptop computer at the kitchen table in the next room, typing email responses to friends, updating them on Ben's condition.

It was still rough going, she was telling them, and it was too early to know if the treatments he was receiving would ultimately provide a cure. His doctors had reason for cautious optimism though May never believed they were totally honest with her.

Ben could be difficult on days he was to be transported to the hospital, and it was only because Kane was allowed to accompany him that he was eventually persuaded to get in the car. He wanted it all to be over. Often the radiation, which now left him without hair, also left him nauseous and weak, but Kane was with him, and his companionship gave the boy, in some unexplainable way, courage no human could provide.

Before leaving, Elizabeth joined her brother, sitting beside him as she rested an arm behind him on the top of the sofa, careful not to make physical contact. He had regressed in his autistic condition to a point he could no longer stand to be touched, and it was always difficult for her to refrain from hugging him, especially now as he sat beside her, helpless and fragile.

"I'm going now," she told him. "I'll see you later."

"Therapy dog appointment?" he asked, only half interested.

"Not exactly," she answered, "Remember the little girl whose father died? Well, I'm going to his funeral."

"Then you'd better take Kane with you," Ben said. "The little girl probably needs him."

"You need him, too," she reminded him.

"Yeah," Ben agreed after thinking a moment, "but I get him all the time. If her dad died, maybe Kane will help her feel better inside, like he does me. Take him with you."

Kane looked up at his boy, then at Elizabeth. The dog felt the same tug at his heart that she felt.

Zach Burton's funeral was a simple graveside service attended by only a handful of mourners, including his estranged wife and daughter. His parents had been deceased for many years, and he had lost contact with his only sister. He hadn't cultivated many friendships since his departure from the Police Department and though the two of them had not been in touch for some time, his old friend Rob Martinez, dressed in his police uniform, stood among the few who turned up to pay last respects.

Elizabeth and Kane stood close to Becky, whose hand rested on his back throughout the ceremony. Many of the words the non-denominational minister spoke meant nothing to the dog, but he vaguely understood the purpose of the occasion, having been present at a similar gathering over a year ago. So he focused on soothing Becky, whose tears were flowing freely. He thought of Ben and the little girl beside him, and he wished, more than anything, that he could make them both smile again.

When the service had concluded, the attendees passed in front of Pauline and Becky to offer their condolences.

"I'm so sorry Zach and I drifted apart these past few years," Rob said as he took her hand.

"I doubt it was your fault," she replied with a smile. "Friendships were something he found difficult to maintain after he left the department. A few people are coming over to the apartment for a bite to eat. Would you care to join us?"

"There's nothing I'd like better," he replied, "but I've got to get back to the station. I'll drop by and see you in the next few days though, if that's okay."

"You're always welcome," she told him.

As he started to step back from her, Pauline's demeanor suddenly changed.

"In fact," she said, grabbing his arm. "There's something I need to talk to you about. Something about Zach. I don't know who else to turn to. I . . . ."

She was interrupted by three friends who surrounded her as they offered condolences.

Waiting for a chance to continue their conversation, Rob felt a slight tug on his sleeve. It was Becky, who had stood and was now hugging him.

"Thank you for helping me," she said, her eyes moist.

Rob returned the hug and struggled to find some words of comfort. As he embraced the girl, he spotted Elizabeth, who was standing nearby. He nodded to her, and she acknowledged him with a smile. Becky turned her attention back to Kane, and

Rob, seeing that Pauline was still occupied, approached Elizabeth.

"It's very nice to see you again. And Kane, too," he said, gesturing toward the dog. "I've been reading up on his history. Very impressive. No wonder he led us to Zach."

"Well, he may not have the same level of intelligence my grandfather gave him," Elizabeth said, "but he's still a pretty smart dog."

There was an awkward silence as he tried to think of something else to say to her. He wanted to know her better. Embarrassed, he turned to leave, but stopped and turned back.

"Say, I've got an idea," he said. "I thought I might pick up Becky in a couple of days and take her someplace, you know, to sort of cheer her up. How about you and Kane coming along? Your brother too, if he's well enough."

Nearby, Kane looked up at the sound of his name and tilted his head slightly.

"It doesn't involve chasing bad guys in your police car, does it?" Elizabeth asked after giving the offer some thought.

"Oh, no," he said with a laugh. "I'll be off duty. We'll find something fun to do."

"I'd love to," she replied, pulling her phone from her purse. "Shall we exchange numbers?"

As they finished their exchange, Pauline, who had managed to pull away from the other guests, joined them.

"Rob, as I was saying . . . ." she began.

Sensing that she was intruding on a personal conversation, Elizabeth started to excuse herself.

"No, please," Pauline stopped her. "It's okay."

"Rob," she continued, "There's something not right about Zach's death. I mean, something about the circumstances. We were separated, but it was never about drugs. I do know that about him. He didn't take drugs. I know he didn't. They didn't even find any sign of drugs in his body."

"I know, Pauline," Rob said. He wanted to comfort her, but he thought she needed to know the facts. "But they think he must have been dealing. They found . . . ."

"That's bullshit!" she responded angrily. "Becky was with him that night. He would never endanger her by putting her in that situation. Never! There's something screwy about the whole mess."

Rob hugged her close as she began sobbing.

"Mommy?" Becky said as she joined them, starting to cry herself.

Pauline knelt beside her daughter, and the two of them comforted one another.

Regaining her composure, Pauline stood, holding Becky's hand.

"Please," she said to Rob. "Is there anything you can do? Anyone that can give us some answers?"

"I'll see if I can find out something more," he assured her. "I'll talk to you again in a few days. I can't promise anything, but . . . ."

Kane was close enough to hear Pauline as she grabbed Rob and whispered in his ear. Her words caused the fur on the dog's neck to stand on end.

"I'm afraid," she heard him whisper. "*I'm afraid for Becky!*"

71

CHAPTER ELEVEN

Later that day, his mother at his side, Ben slept in his chair in the Pediatric Oncology Department as his treatment was being administered, while Elizabeth and Kane moved about the room visiting the other young patients. Sharing good cheer and smiles, Elizabeth coaxed the dog to perform a few perfunctory tricks.

Performing tricks (or "behaviors" as he preferred to think of them) was something he generally considered beneath his dignity, but Kane was willing to submit to her request when he saw the joy it brought to the children he visited. Their happiness made *him* happy, and soon he would find himself so caught up in the laughs and cheers that he would often wind up exceeding the repertoire of behaviors Elizabeth generally requested of him. To the delight of each child, Elizabeth handed each one a specially prepared trading card to keep, which bore Kane's image and statistics.

When Kane and his family were exiting the hospital building upon completion of Ben's treatment, they passed a young couple with their six-year-old son in the front lobby waiting room. The boy was sitting in a wheelchair, his head hanging to the side, his eyes staring blankly into space, his hands lying lifeless in his lap. His position indicated he had little or no control of his body. The expression on the parents' faces, weary though they must have been, nevertheless reflected their courage and their love for the boy.

Elizabeth asked her mother to wait a few minutes, and she led Kane toward the family. Introducing them both, she asked permission for Kane to visit their son. Kane approached as he always did when meeting a child, his tail wagging as he looked up into the boy's face, and he stood next to the wheelchair as he had been taught to do so that the boy could pet him if he wished. He was not within the child's field of vision, however, so the boy's expression remained unchanged.

Elizabeth gently took the child's limp hand and guided his palm along the soft fur on Kane's back and then over his ears and down his long muzzle. As this occurred, a sparkle in the boy's eyes could be perceived, and Kane lifted his front paws to the arm of the wheelchair, pulling his body into an elevated position, standing on his rear legs. The boy's father tilted his son's head so that he could focus on the dog.

Elizabeth released the boy's hand, but it remained in the thick, radiant white rough that encircled Kane's neck, clutching the fur tightly. As their eyes met, an expression of wonder and joy spread over the boy's face and Kane continued to wag his tail.

"I'm here, little one," Kane thought. *"I see you. Whenever you feel unhappy or alone or afraid, recall this moment and know that you are loved and know that I'll remember you for as long as I live."*

A full, brilliant, exuberant smile expanded across the boy's face causing his nose to wrinkle and turning his eyes into slits.

His parents had never seen him excited this way and his mother's hand went to her lips as his father quietly wept. Elizabeth, too, was overcome though she tried not to become too emotional in front of the family. As for Kane, this connection helped lift his heart from the depression he had been experiencing, and he wished he could feel this way forever.

At that moment, a nurse appeared and informed the family that the doctor was ready to see their son. As the parents thanked Elizabeth, she placed a trading card into the boy's one good hand, and he clutched it awkwardly to his chest. Kane stepped down from the wheelchair and positioned himself into a bow toward the child before sitting and lifting his front paw in a friendly, goodbye wave. The boy's father turned the wheelchair away and directed it toward the doorway held open by the nurse.

As she was about to enter the doorway behind them, the mother suddenly stopped and rushed back to Kane. Kneeling next to him, she encircled his neck with her arms, and she placed her cheek next to his face, as she kept her eyes tightly shut. After nearly a minute in this position, she gathered her strength and stood, rushing to catch up with her husband and son before the door closed behind her.

Returning to her side with Kane, Elizabeth noticed a slight smile on her mother's face.

"OK, I see what this is all about," May said to her with an air of humility. "Good for you. And good for you, Kane."

CHAPTER TWELVE

Elizabeth had kept her decision to participate in her new assignment at the Los Angeles jails a secret from her mother. It wasn't until the day of her first visit that she broke the news to her and she tried her best to make it sound exciting and challenging while downplaying the danger. Ultimately, once again facing her daughter's unwavering determination (stubbornness, she often thought of it), May was forced to relent with a shake of her head, hands held high in resignation.

Gathering her purse and car keys, Elizabeth couldn't help but notice the force with which her mother's fingers struck the keys on her computer that sat before her at the kitchen table. With a sigh, Elizabeth placed a comforting arm around her and gave her shoulder a loving hug.

"Thank you, Mom," she whispered in her ear. "I love you."

May softened for a moment before stiffening once again.

"I love you too," she responded, a severe frown on her face. "But how much I love you and how much you love me has nothing to do with your safety."

Her daughter smiled, gave her a soft pat on the back and left the room. May called out to Kane, who stood nearby watching the exchange between mother and daughter with concern. He responded to her summons, and when he stood next to her chair, she turned toward him, and placed a hand on each side of his face, looking sternly into his eyes.

"I'm counting on you, Kane," she whispered to him. "Keep my little girl safe."

The Men's Central Jail in downtown Los Angeles, the largest facility of its kind in the United States, is equipped to house over 5,000 inmates, whose crimes range from minor to major. Inmates at The Twin Towers Correctional Facility next door include those who are being treated for physical or psychological problems and many of the inmates in both facilities are considered highly dangerous and unpredictable. The therapy dog program implemented there, is a unique event in which select handlers and their dogs spend time with them.

Corrections Officer Bert Vega was sliding open the main cell door to admit Elizabeth and Kane into an entryway at the Men's Correctional Facility that led toward several secure doors behind which inmates were confined. Beyond those doors were long hallways lined on one side with jail cells containing one to four inmates. Officer Vega, in his late thirties, was somber but friendly and Kane appreciated the strong sense of security he projected. He often directed his attention toward the dog but remained watchful and protective of Elizabeth and for that Kane was especially grateful as he was particularly apprehensive about her presence in this place.

"We'll try to get around to see as many of them as we can," the officer explained as they walked, "but there won't be time to get to all of them. It's a large facility, as you've already seen."

Elizabeth had obtained her security clearance and had attended a volunteer orientation in which she had been prepared for the work she would be expected to perform as Kane's handler. She was confident in her ability to deal with any situation that might arise, and she felt secure and unafraid in the presence of the jail staff and with the dog at her side.

As he was turning the key in the lock that would take them into a group of jail cells, Officer Vega reminded Elizabeth of the purpose of her visit.

"Some people think bringing therapy dogs to inmates is a reward they don't deserve," he explained. "Even some of our own staff here resent it, especially after they've been attacked by one of them. I guess you could call it a reward, but the purpose is to provide a calming influence. I've seen it for myself. After a visit with the dogs, the inmates are a lot easier to handle."

The security door was swung wide, and Kane and Elizabeth followed him into the hallway before the row of cells. The cell doors were open, and several of prisoners were conversing casually in the hall while others remained in their lockups, playing cards or talking with other inmates, some reading books, and some asleep in their bunks.

It was at first confusing to Kane. He was accustomed to kennels and cages for animals, but he had never before seen humans caged this way. Like the human penchant for killing each other for no apparent reason, it was another of the many inconsistencies in human behavior that puzzled him. Were the people here less than human that they must be kept penned up like dogs? His mind touched on the idea that it must be some sort of punishment such as he remembered as a puppy when he had committed an infraction, and his master sent him to his metal crate and commanded him to remain there until he was allowed to come out. That's what this is, he finally figured. It's punishment. But the men in gray must have done something more severe than merely chewing up a shoe. Like many human behaviors, he was unable to fully make sense of, he tossed aside the need to understand and instead got on with the business at hand.

Elizabeth and Kane quickly adapted to the routine of approaching the door to each cell while Officer Vega asked each occupant if he would like to visit with the dog. In most cases, the inmates were anxious and eagerly accepted Kane into the cell while Elizabeth stood in the doorway, holding onto the end of her dog's leash with both hands, prepared to pull him out of danger if the situation required. It never did. Even those inmates who might have at first appeared menacing, were transformed by the dog's presence as they dropped all pretense of machismo, often kneeling or crouching beside the dog with an enormous smile. They would rough his coat, talk to him cheerfully, and sometimes give him a hug.

Some inmates would not allow themselves to step from behind the solid façade of virile toughness they chose to convey for fear that others would see them as weak. Firmly shaking their heads when offered the opportunity to pet the dog, Elizabeth often found that such a wall was not necessarily unbreakable. Observing the gratification his cell-mates were enjoying, often even the most hardened criminal would eventually find Kane's soft fur and soothing presence just too hard to resist, finally reaching for the dog, tentatively at first, and then with enthusiasm.

Elizabeth was usually not told the crimes the inmates were accused of, and she didn't ask. Nor did she wonder if the inmates were guilty or innocent. It was better not to know, she reasoned and made it easier for her to perform her job without prejudice or judgment. Better to watch and learn from the collie who willingly entered each cell, wagging his tail and greeting everyone with the same humility and warmth. It was one of many virtues, Elizabeth considered, humans would do well to learn from a dog.

Though Elizabeth was aware of the occasional lustful stare cast in her direction, she had prepared herself by simply ignoring them until their attention was directed toward the dog.

"You can never be too cautious," Vega warned her, "but you're relatively safe in here. They know you're a volunteer, not an authority figure like the deputies and me, so they don't resent you. In fact, they appreciate what you're doing for them, and if one of them should try to harm either you or Kane, the offender would have to face the wrath of the other inmates. They'd all be afraid of being denied their privileges because of the behavior of one guy. They'd make the guy pay."

Passing from cell to cell, Kane became more relaxed and he relished the attention and goodwill each man conveyed.

Approaching a group of three inmates who stood conversing outside a cell, Elizabeth offered them the opportunity to pet Kane. One of them, a very large, bearded, heavily-built, brooding, black man withdrew from the group and stood by himself nearby, turning his head away, refusing to take part in the visit. Elizabeth was curious and she watched him as she answered the same questions she was asked by nearly everyone she had met.

"Is this a male or female?"

"He's a male."

"What's his name?"

"Kane."

"How old is he?"

"Nine years old."

"What kind of dog is he?"

"Collie. You know, like Lassie?"

"Lassie! That's what I thought. Hey, Lassie, Timmy's in the well! You'd better go save him!"

This would always be followed by laughter and Elizabeth would do her best to laugh with them, though she'd heard a variation of the same remark countless times before.

Finally, she wished the men well and proceeded to another cell and another group of men. As she passed the bearded man who stood down the hall, she saw him turn his head back toward the direction she had traveled, to avoid looking at either her or Kane.

"Would you care to . . . ," she started to ask as he stepped away from her.

The man said nothing as he deliberately continued to ignore her.

Elizabeth looked at Officer Vega, but he just shook his head and shrugged.

"Excuse me, sir," she called after the mysterious man. He stopped but kept his back to her.

As she approached him, the other two men moved into a nearby cell to play cards. Vega stood behind her, watching cautiously.

When she was near him, he called out to her over his shoulder, still refusing to look at her.

"Keep that damn dog away from me," he told her coldly.

"Sure, of course," she assured him in a calm voice. "But, well, I just can't help but wonder why you won't have anything to do with him. Are you afraid of him?"

"I ain't afraid of no *dog!*" he exclaimed.

"Then what's the problem?" she asked.

The man stood for a moment, immobile and unresponsive. Suddenly he walked into his cell, slamming the door behind him.

Officer Vega touched her arm and jerked his head over his shoulder to indicate that they'd better move on. Elizabeth and Kane turned to follow him, but they were only a few steps away when the inmate's door was quickly opened. Turning back, she expected to see him walk out, but he remained inside, out of view. When there was no further response, she started to leave.

"I don't want to get near the dog," he called to her quietly, the emotion building in his voice. "I had a dog. She meant everything to me. Two weeks ago they came to arrest me, and they shot her. You understand? My dog died, and I blame myself. I can't . . . I can't . . . ."

Elizabeth heard a sob, and the cell door was slammed shut again.

Kane pulled at the leash in an attempt to go to the man, but Elizabeth stopped him.

"No," she told him. "Not now, Kane. Come."

They turned and left the area.

Leaving the row of cells, they entered a large connecting hallway and Kane reflected on the man they had just encountered. Like Elizabeth, he had been puzzled by his reluctance to interact, but he could sense that his reason for doing so was an emotional one.

A door leading into the area through which they were passing was opened. A tall, thin, wiry, black prisoner, his hands and feet in chains, was escorted through by five deputies. He wore his hair closely cropped and sported a short beard. His body was covered with crude tattoos and his lips were locked in an eerie, perpetual smile.

"Walking!" one of the deputies called out.

Officer Vega signaled for Elizabeth and Kane to give a wide berth to the group as they passed and Kane became aware of a faintly familiar smell emanating from the dangerous looking detainee. He remembered where he had smelled that odor before.

"Rodney Hawkins," Vega whispered to Elizabeth after he was led by them and out another door. "He's the guy . . . ."

"It's probably best I don't know who he is," Elizabeth interrupted, holding up a hand.

"Well," the officer said with a chuckle, "you probably won't have any choice. He's been in all the news. He's the guy they arrested for killing that ex-cop last week in some kind of drug deal gone bad. You must have heard about it. The mayor's been talking about it. Big story."

Kane saw Elizabeth tense up.

"Will we be visiting him?" Elizabeth asked as they continued their walk.

"Maybe," Vega shrugged. "They're moving him next door to give his bad back some medical attention. You might see him over there. Unless you don't want to. You never have to spend time with anyone you don't want to."

"I think not," Elizabeth said, suppressing a shudder.

CHAPTER THIRTEEN

Hoping to escape notice, Rob Martinez cautiously entered the Homicide Department, a cluttered office space not far down the hall from the office where he reported at Headquarters. Surveying the room he was relieved to notice that everyone was focused on their work and paid no attention to him. Rob was particularly comforted to find that Detective Mosher was not among them.

At the back of the room he recognized a detective seated at a desk cluttered with paperwork and photographs, talking on the telephone. He paid no notice to Rob who approached and stood behind him, smiling. The man was in his mid-forties, prematurely balding, and the patches of tousled hair on the side of his head, like the goatee on his face, were peppered with gray. The tip of the brightly colored tie he wore loosely around his neck stopped short of his slacks that were tightly secured with a belt below a bulging stomach. The lenses of the reading glasses perched low on his nose were smudged and provided only minimal help to his tired-looking eyes. The pack of cigarettes barely visible beneath a stack of reports before him confirmed what Rob expected. His old friend hadn't changed. He pulled up a chair from an empty desk nearby and sat next to him.

The frazzled detective turned to see who had joined him. Casting a quick, annoyed look at Rob, he returned to his phone call before acknowledging him with a friendly smile of recognition. Eventually managing to extract himself from what was apparently an irritating caller, he slammed the phone into its cradle and sighed long and hard.

"How's Homicide treating you these days, Detective Ralston?" the officer asked cheerfully.

"It's murder around here, haven't I ever told you that?" Ralston answered sarcastically.

"Yeah, you've used that one before, Danny," Rob said with a friendly pat on his friend's knee.

"That guy must have left his brain someplace for repairs!" Danny shouted, gesturing back at the phone.

"I hope you're not letting this place get to you," Rob laughed.

"Nah," his friend said, snorting. "What's not to like? I got fun, adventure, great people to work with."

"You mean, like Detective Mosher?"

Danny had been leaning back in his chair, but at the mention of Mosher's name, he moved to an upright position.

"He's okay," he shrugged, "just kissing up to whoever he thinks can get him promoted. What's on your mind, Rob?"

"I got a favor to ask," Rob said, lowering his voice.

"Of course you do," Danny replied, rolling his eyes. "Why else would you come to see me? Wait. Let me think. Don't you already owe me for past favors? Is this gonna get me in trouble?"

"Zach Burton. You're working on that one, right?"

"Too bad about Zach."

Danny paused, lost in a memory he had of the exiled cop. After a moment, he searched through a stack of folders before withdrawing one and tossing it in the middle of his desk.

"I don't need to tell you this is none of your business, right?" he said, looking over the rims of his glasses at the officer.

"It's pretty much a closed case at this point, isn't it?" Rob asked.

"Pretty much," the detective replied. "Except this damn file sure gets pulled out a lot. People coming in here looking at it that ain't got no business."

"You mean, people like me?"

"And some that should have less reason than you. Then there's that surveillance footage from the liquor store went missing before it could be claimed. And his kid that witnessed the murder."

"Wait a minute," Martinez interrupted. "Who's been looking at the file? What about the surveillance footage? What did his daughter see?"

Danny grabbed his head. "You're confusing my mind, man. So many questions and I don't have all the answers. I need a smoke."

He ruffled through several papers on his desk a moment before Rob spotted the cigarette pack, pulled it from beneath the clutter and tossed it on the desk in front of him.

"I hope you're a speed reader," Danny said, grabbing the pack and stuffing it in his shirt pocket as he stood to leave. "Mosher could be back any minute. He probably wouldn't like you."

He stopped for a moment, eyeing his old friend.

"No," he said as he walked away, "I'm sure he wouldn't like you."

Taking a quick glance around the room, Rob anxiously opened the folder on the desk as he seated himself in Danny's chair. Placing the contents in his lap, he pulled his camera phone from his pocket. Using the desktop to conceal his actions, he quickly leafed through several pages, stopping periodically to take a picture, looking up occasionally to ensure that no one was watching him.

Before he had a chance to complete his review, however, Danny came rushing back in, nodding over his shoulder. Rob recognized the signal and promptly closed the file and shoved it amid a pile of other documents on the desk, then quickly stood and headed for the doorway. He circled the desks nearest the walls, hoping he wouldn't be noticed by Mosher when he entered.

Danny reached his desk and threw down his cigarette pack just as Detective Mosher strode in. Much to Rob's relief, the detective made his way down the center aisle toward his desk. Keeping his back toward him, Rob made fast his exit.

Mosher had removed his jacket and was proceeding to hang it on his chair when he happened to notice the back of the uniformed officer who had just left the room and was headed down the hall. He watched him depart, his curiosity building, before looking at Danny, seated at the desk beside him.

Danny quickly snatched a piece of paper from his desk and handed it to the detective.

"Your wife called," Danny told him. "Sounded important."

Mosher's attention was still on the door.

"Is that who I think it is?" he said as he turned to look at Danny.

"Hmm?" Danny replied, assuming the best look of innocence he could muster. He knew it failed to convince.

Throwing the note he had been handed into his trash can, Mosher grabbed the telephone on his desk and dialed.

"This is Detective Mosher, Homicide," he grumbled into the mouthpiece. "I want to talk to Officer Martinez' supervisor."

CHAPTER FOURTEEN

Elizabeth and Pauline were seated across from each other sipping coffee in the comfortably decorated front room of Pauline's two-bedroom condominium while Kane and Becky amused themselves in her room. Pauline had extended an invitation for an evening visit after giving in to her daughter's endless pleas.

"It was tough trying to carry on after Zach and I split," Pauline told Elizabeth.

"But you never divorced?" Elizabeth asked.

"No, no," she said, firmly shaking her head. "We loved each other too much ever to do that. I guess we were both hoping someday we'd be together again. But he was obsessed with that damn investigation, and it just got really bad, and I couldn't live with it anymore. So, when I'd finally had enough, I told him to go get it out of his system. Then, when he found all the answers he was looking for, and when he was ready to lead a normal life, I promised him I'd be right there, waiting for him. Well, he got a job with a security company and I found a job doing accounting, and I just waited for him to come home."

She toyed with a tissue as her voice broke.

"I shouldn't have made him leave," she continued. "We should have had more time together."

"You can't blame yourself," Elizabeth consoled her. "Are you going to do okay? Financially?"

"Fortunately for Becky," Pauline said, nodding, "it looks like his life insurance policy will help us along and even help pay for her college some day. 'Course, both of us would rather he was around to see her graduate."

The door to Becky's room was ajar, and from where the two ladies were sitting they could see her seated on the floor at the foot of her bed, a book open in her lap as she read to Kane, who was lying next to her.

"The girl does love her books," Pauline said, smiling and shaking her head as she watched her daughter. "Zach would come over at night as often as he could, and he'd always bring her some book he'd picked up at some old used book store. Then they'd sit down and read it together. Dog stories are her favorite. She must have a hundred of them in there in her bookcase."

"Kane's favorite kind of story," Elizabeth said with a wink, and the two of them laughed together.

In her room, Becky paged through the book she held in her lap. Though most of the words contained there were above her comprehension level, she nevertheless managed to relate the story to Kane, substituting her own story to accompany the pictures. Kane listened attentively, and he found the sound of her voice calming and comforting.

"The end," she said, closing the cover of the book. "Would you like to hear another one? I've got lots of dog books. Even some about collies."

Standing before the bookcase which sat against a wall near her bed, she returned the book held in her hand by wedging it between several others. Running a finger along the spines of her collection, she searched for just the exact story to read to her new friend.

"Let's see," she whispered. "Where is that book? Oh, here it is."

Becky pulled a large book from the shelf and examined the cover. The book was worn and aged, and its cover featured a beautiful color illustration of a collie.

"See?" Becky said, showing Kane the cover before attempting to read the title. "'The Heart of a Dog' by Al-bert . . . ummh, Pays . . . Payson T-T . . . Well, I can't read his full name. Anyway, my dad brought me this book just before . . . ." Her voice trailed off.

"Well," she said, "I don't think I want to read this book tonight."

She started to return the book to the bookcase when something fell to the floor from between its pages. It was a sealed envelope.

"Oh!" Becky exclaimed as she hastily gathered up the envelope. She placed it back between the pages of the book before sliding it back into the bookcase on a shelf at her eye level.

Kneeling next to the collie, she pulled him close.

"Kane!" she whispered into his ear confidentially. "You must promise me that you won't ever tell anyone you saw that envelope. It's a secret. My daddy made me swear on a stack of Bibles that I would never show it to anyone. Ever!"

Becky held up her right hand.

"Raise your right hand, Kane," she said to him. Kane lifted his right paw.

"Swear to me you will never, *ever* tell anyone about that envelope!"

Kane held his paw high, and Becky studied his face intently.

"Well," she said after a while. "Okay. I guess I can trust you."

In the next room, the adults were sharing a laugh when the doorbell rang, and Pauline stood to answer it, wondering aloud who it was.

Securing the chain security lock, Pauline cautiously cracked the door just wide enough to see her visitor's face.

"Missus Burton?" asked a friendly male voice.

Pauline nodded tentatively.

"I'm Richard Teller. I'm Executive Assistant to Mayor Robbins. I hope I'm not intruding, but the mayor asked me to stop by to offer my condolences on the loss of your husband. May I come in for a moment? I'll only be a minute."

Pauline unhitched the chain and guardedly stood aside to allow her visitor to enter.

Richard Teller was a short, round, balding man dressed in an immaculate tan suit and a bright green tie. He sported a broad, insincere smile which he had mastered during many political campaigns on behalf of the mayor.

"Good evening, Ma'am," he said, nodding to Elizabeth as he took in the contents of the room. He held Pauline's hand tightly with both of his.

"Missus Burton," he addressed her, his smile unwavering, "Mayor Robbins wants you to know how personally sorry he is for the loss of your husband, and I would like to convey his heartfelt sympathy to you during this difficult time. He also wants you to know that if there is anything he can do for you, please don't hesitate to ask."

Pauline looked at him askance. "I didn't think the mayor even knew who my husband was."

"Oh, Missus Burton," Teller said with a condescending chuckle, still holding her hand. "Our mayor has always been committed to the men and women who serve our city, and he takes a personal interest in each and every one."

"Mister Teller," Pauline said skeptically, "my husband was terminated by the department some time ago."

"Of course," he replied, finally releasing her hand and patting her arm, "but that doesn't make one bit of difference. Not to the mayor and, I might add, not to me."

From her bedroom, Becky could hear the voices in the next room. She slid across the carpet to the half-opened doorway. Peeking around the door to see who had come to visit, she suddenly froze and held her breath, as her heart began to pound.

Noticing the abrupt change in her demeanor, Kane joined her at the door, but she hurriedly pushed herself away and moved back into a narrow area between the side of the bed and her bedroom wall. There she sat huddled in the corner, her eyes wide.

Kane recognized the look on her face. He'd seen it the night he first met her at the police station. As he moved closer to her, she promptly threw her arms around him and held him close. Kane could feel her body trembling. He licked her cheek.

"It's okay," he wanted to tell her. "Just hold me close, and I will keep you safe and warm. I promise to protect you with my life."

"Even though your husband wasn't with the department at the time of his death," continued Teller in the next room, "we are nevertheless grateful for his dedication and his commitment."

There was an awkward silence as he seemed to expect a response.

"You know," he said rubbing his neck, "I wonder if he ever uncovered anything. I mean, anything the authorities ought to look into. The mayor was just wondering the other day about that. It would sure help us track down . . . ."

"Mister Teller," Pauline interrupted, "I've been through this numerous times with the investigators. I told them, and I will tell you. Once. I have no knowledge of any evidence my husband might have left behind, and there's been a thorough search made of his apartment and mine. So now, if you'll excuse me."

"Oh, of course," he said in a reassuring tone of voice. "I'm sorry for the intrusion, but I only hope you'll remember the mayor's offer and if there is ever anything we can do, here's my card . . . ."

Pauline accepted his card but cut him off as she reached to open the front door.

"Please thank Mayor Robbins for me," she told him, "but right now everyone can help me best by just leaving my daughter and me alone."

Teller glanced in Elizabeth's direction before flashing his broad smile and, with a nod of his head to Pauline, he turned to leave. She rolled her eyes and shook her head as he walked down the walkway. She was about to close the door when she saw someone else headed her way.

"Now who in the hell . . . ?" she started to wonder before her new visitor came into view. He had to walk past Teller before she recognized him.

"Rob!" she exclaimed with surprise.

He was dressed casually and greeted her warmly.

"Sure is good to see you," she said, giving him a warm hug. "Come on in. Elizabeth and I were just having a chat. You met before, right?"

"Sure we have," Elizabeth said, extending her hand as he entered the room. "Always good to see you! How you been?"

"Can't complain," he replied with a shrug and a friendly smile as he glanced around the room. "Where's Becky?"

"Oh, she's off in her room with Kane and her books," Pauline replied, nodding toward the bedroom. "Sit down. Let me pour you a cup of coffee."

Pauline headed to the kitchen.

"I'll bet Kane is smart enough to read a book to Becky," he said sitting next to Elizabeth. "From what I've read, he's a pretty extraordinary character."

"We're just glad that part of his life is behind us now," she replied.

"How's your brother?" he asked.

Elizabeth forced a smile. "It's too early to know if the treatments are doing any good. I don't know which is harder on him, the cancer or the cure. But somehow he manages to deal with it. He's probably handling it better than my mother."

"Why do our children have to be tested?" Pauline wondered, as she re-entered the room and handed Rob a cup of coffee. "And where do they find the strength to deal with it? I wish I had some of that grit."

She shook her head as she sat in an armchair.

"I guess we just have to try to stay positive," Elizabeth said, "and take comfort in one another. I think that's something I've learned from Kane. He's helped Ben a lot."

The three of them sat quietly sipping their coffee for a moment.

"Who was that I saw on the way in?" Rob asked, breaking the silence.

Pauline handed him Teller's card.

"Oh yeah," Rob said, remembering he had seen him at Captain Takimoto's office. "What did he want, if you don't mind my asking?"

"Same as they all want," Pauline told him. "Looking for evidence from Zach's investigation. I thought now that he's dead I wouldn't hear anything more about that."

"Hmmm," Rob pondered. "I wonder why the mayor's office would be interested."

"You didn't just come over here for a friendly visit did you, Rob?" Pauline asked, changing the subject.

"Yeah," he replied. glancing back and forth between the two of them. "I need to ask both of you to keep this information to yourselves. I'm snooping into areas I'm not allowed to go, and I'm not even sure what can of worms I'm opening up here but . . . ."

He looked at Pauline apprehensively before continuing. "I think you might be right. There's a lot of loose pieces that don't all fit together."

Pauline closed her eyes and sighed.

"I knew it," she said.

"What kind of pieces?" Elizabeth asked.

"First of all, his autopsy," Rob answered. "No sign of drugs in his system, and I think you're right about the drug dealing, Pauline. Why would he come by here and pick up Becky if he was planning to make a sale that night? And why would the guy who killed him leave the drugs behind?"

Rob shook his head. "No. That packet of drugs was planted. It had to be."

Elizabeth reached for Pauline's hand and held it as Rob spoke.

"The guy they arrested for the murder, name's Hawkins," he continued. "It was pretty easy. Detective Mosher knew right where to find him. They matched the gun in his possession to the bullets that killed Zach.

"And that drug dealing bull has no evidence to back it up. No evidence anywhere of any drug money. No evidence of any kind that would stand up to that accusation. Sure, he was in contact with some pretty shady characters, but it was all in connection with that investigation he wouldn't let go of."

"What was he trying to investigate, anyway? Elizabeth asked.

"Drug trafficking," Rob replied. "At some point, he got frustrated with the lack of cooperation he was getting from the department. He started stepping on toes and he got fired. But he was convinced he was close to busting up a pretty big ring, and he just couldn't let it go."

"Then it would be a pretty safe bet to assume he was killed because of it," Elizabeth speculated.

"A pretty safe bet," Rob agreed. "But it may have involved more than Hawkins and his gang."

"Corrupt cops?" Pauline asked.

"Maybe a few," he replied, shaking his head. "I haven't found any evidence of it yet, though I'd guess there has to be somebody on the inside. But there's been a lot of interest from others. Somebody outside of law enforcement. I don't know who yet."

Shifting to the edge of his seat, he asked Pauline, "Did Zach ever tell you anything at all about the case? Are you sure he didn't leave behind any files?"

"The only thing he ever told me was that he was on to something pretty big," she told him. "Nothing beyond that. Detective Mosher and his crew already asked me about that. They tore up his apartment. They took his computer, too. Then they came back and asked me again if I knew anything."

"Funny thing," Rob said, looking at the floor, "his computer wasn't entered into evidence. Could just be sloppy reporting, I don't know. See, it's that kind of thing that looks suspicious."

"So where do we go from here?" Pauline asked.

"*You* don't do anything. I'll keep snooping around, but I've got to be discreet. My superiors will have my head if they find out. So you just sit tight and don't talk to anybody."

He stood to leave, then stopped abruptly.

"At the funeral," he said to Pauline, "you said you thought Becky might be in some kind of danger. What makes you think that?"

"I don't know," she replied, rubbing her arms with her hands as if she felt a chill. "Something I can't put my finger on. All the questions the deputies kept asking me, kind of gave me the creeps. First, they kept asking me if Zach left any papers with me, if he had a lock box or anything like that. Then they asked Becky the same questions. They really seemed interested in her. What worries me most is the things Becky saw that night. She's a witness. That's why I think she's in danger."

Rob nodded his understanding, then reached into his jacket pocket, withdrew a card and handed it to her.

"My number's on there," he told her before handing another card to Elizabeth. Keep a close watch on her. But if you have even an inkling of worry, call me immediately, and I'll be here in a flash. You promise?"

Pauline nodded.

"And if you can think of anyplace he might have hidden something," he continued, "don't let anyone but me know about it. Understand?"

"Of course," Pauline promised.

"Good night, Becky," he yelled toward the bedroom door.

There was no response.

"Sweetheart?" Pauline called out. Still no answer. She turned and entered her daughter's bedroom, followed by Elizabeth and Rob.

They found her huddled in the corner, holding onto Kane.

Pauline lifted Becky onto the bed and gave her a reassuring hug and Kane took the liberty of jumping onto the bed to be beside her.

"She's trembling," Pauline said to the others, checking her head for a temperature. "What's wrong, baby? Can you tell us?"

Becky couldn't speak.

"Perhaps she's had a flashback," Elizabeth guessed, then leaned forward, stroking the top of Becky's head. "It's okay, sweetheart, Kane is here, remember? He'll keep you safe."

"It's going to take time," Rob said.

"I don't want to talk right now," Becky said softly, as she pulled away from her mother's embrace. "Come on, Kane. I'll read you another story."

Kane joined her as she sat on the floor at the foot of the bed and picked up a book.

The adults remained in the room a while longer until Rob finally excused himself and let himself out the front door.

"Tell you what," Elizabeth said to Pauline. "Maybe Becky would like it if Kane stayed the night with her. You think your landlord would mind?"

"Oh, my dear," Pauline replied with a smile. "He doesn't have to know about it. That would be so wonderful. "

"I'll pick him up in the morning," Elizabeth told her. "And if you'd like, I'll bring him back for another sleepover in a day or two."

Pauline hugged her and the two of them returned to the front room and talked late into the evening.

When it was bedtime, Kane waited patiently as Becky's mother tucked her in. When Pauline turned off the light and closed the door, he climbed up close to Becky, looking into her face until she fell asleep.

CHAPTER FIFTEEN

"I'll take your sidearm and your badge," Sergeant Freeman demanded as he sat behind his desk at Police Headquarters.

"Sir?" replied Rob, standing before his desk.

"The department was willing to give you a pass for leapfrogging over chain of command when you went straight to the captain to request to join the Burton murder investigation," Freeman said, "your exemplary performance up to this point earned you a few credits. But now you're poking your nose into something that's none of your business. You'd do well to take a few weeks off so you can clear your mind of all responsibility except those to which you have been officially assigned. You're being placed on administrative leave. Understood?"

Rob knew this was coming, but he hoped he could talk his way out of disciplinary action with the facts.

"Sir," he pleaded, "there's a lot more to this case than anybody seems to realize."

"Anybody but you?" Freeman said skeptically. "Look, I know Burton was your friend but the men assigned to this case are experienced professionals. They'll do their jobs. Now, you could have received stiffer disciplinary action than a mere two weeks off, but like I said, your record has been spotless. Just be advised that your credits are all used up now. So just walk away from this case and see if you can't start earning some of those credits back."

Rob opened his mouth to speak but was quickly interrupted.

"That will be all, Officer," Freeman said firmly.

Reluctantly, Rob unpinned his badge and unholstered his weapon. Removing the clip from the gun, he placed them on his sergeant's desk before he turned and walked silently out of the office. In a way, Rob thought, his suspension came at a convenient time. Now he would have more time to proceed with his "unauthorized" investigation. From the police station, he drove directly to the corner liquor store where Zach had dropped off his daughter on the night of his death.

That morning, before leaving for the jail, Elizabeth checked in with her mother, who was packing her laptop computer into a bag she used to transport it. May was talking excitedly, sometimes angrily, about her research on childhood cancer. She was wholly absorbed with the facts she was uncovering about Ben's disease and was now resolved to do everything she could do to bring those facts to the public's attention.

"I was one of those people," she said to Elizabeth as she searched for her keys. "Childhood cancer had nothing to do with me. My children are healthy. No, it's not until it happens to you that you even give it a thought. And the politicians! Each year they give less money for cancer research than it takes to make a modestly budgeted action movie. It's sickening, Elizabeth!"

"You're right, Mom," Elizabeth agreed as she took her hand. "And I want you to know how proud I am that you're trying to change that."

May paused to catch her breath. "Yeah, well . . . I'm going to make this my life's work now. I owe it not just to Ben, but to all those kids."

Ben was seated on the couch in the front room, solemnly putting on his shoes as Kane sat before him, watching him with concern. Elizabeth had repeatedly offered to discontinue attending the therapy dog visits that so often took Kane from his side. As Ben's physical condition worsened, she had eliminated her visits to all locations except one weekly visit to the men's jail and an occasional assignment to the Children's Advocacy Center. This allowed Ben and Kane more time together, but it was apparent to her that Kane was deeply troubled by his inability to be with the boy every minute.

For his part, Ben had become increasingly generous with Kane's time. As he became more dependent on the dog, so grew his need to share his friend with anyone who needed him. Ben believed it was meaningful and he felt tremendous pride in the work his dog was doing. Each time Elizabeth returned after one of her visits, he wanted to know every detail, and it made him happy when she related the joy Kane was giving to others.

"Come along, boy," Elizabeth called to Kane as she opened the front door. "We've got an important job to do today at the jail."

"You go ahead, Kane," Ben said pointing to the door. "You teach all those bad men that they need to be good people so that when they get out of jail, they won't get into any more trouble."

Kane lowered his head and walked out the door with Elizabeth as Ben watched him go.

"Good boy, Kane," he called after him meekly.

That day Kane and Elizabeth were scheduled to visit the Twin Towers Jail, so named because it consists of two connected towers which house maximum-security inmates, those with health issues as well as a significant portion of the county's mental health internees.

As he and Elizabeth were escorted through a confusing maze of hallways and connecting security chambers and up and down several elevators, Kane was immediately aware of two significant differences between the Twin Towers facility and the Men's Central Jail next door. There were no bars on any of the enclosures which were secured with heavy doors containing unbreakable windows. Their first job was at a facility in an open area before three separate "pods" enclosed behind ceiling-high windows, constantly being monitored by staff.

Kane and Elizabeth were accompanied by Corrections Officer Schafter, a young, cheerful woman in her mid-forties who generated a strong sense of trust and reliability, characteristics for which Kane was always grateful.

As soon as the therapy dog team entered the open area, many inmates would rush to the windows of their pod to see the dog, pleading for the opportunity to pet him.

"Look at the way that dog walks," one of them said. "Yeah, that's a show dog for sure."

The limitations placed on visitor and inmate during the visits were based on the safety and behavior of the occupants of each pod. In some instances, Kane and Elizabeth were admitted inside the to visit inmates, many of whom were chained to tables. Others were only permitted to touch the dog through an open food tray slot located in the center of the heavily secured door leading into the pod. Kane would stand on his hind legs, resting his front paws on the ledge of the tray slot while inmates would kneel and reach awkwardly through the opening, gently stroking his fur and scratching his neck, talking to him and asking Elizabeth questions. A line was formed along the large glass front of the enclosure, and each inmate would patiently wait his turn to touch Kane, straining to see him over the shoulder of the individual standing in front. No inmate monopolized the time spent with the dog and after a minute or two would step away from the door and allow the next inmate his turn.

Elizabeth couldn't help but be moved by the scene before her. Some of the men would laugh with joy, some remained solemn and occasionally even tearful at this first opportunity, some for perhaps months or years, to exchange physical affection with another living creature. Each man would express gratitude for the chance to touch Kane before leaving the door to allow the next inmate his turn.

"God bless you, Ma'am," they would say with a smile and a nod of the head, often wiping away a tear.

Kane wasn't sure what this ceremony was about, but he knew he was needed. He didn't know why any of them were there in that place and he didn't care. He didn't judge them, and they knew it, and for that reason, the visits were important to them.

Elizabeth and Kane worked out a routine they would perform in the open area before leaving each group of pods. As the inmates gathered behind the windows looking out onto the open space at Kane, he would sit and wave goodbye to them with his paw. Even the most hardened criminal would laugh and merrily wave back to the dog.

"Goodbye, Kane! Come see us again soon!" they would call out.

For those few seconds, Elizabeth believed, each man was a child again.

"If you're up for it," Officer Schafter said to her as they continued to their next destination, "we'd like you to spend some time with one of our Level Ten inmates. Level Ten is what we call our more complex cases, men who are difficult to handle or who may have attacked a deputy. We keep them isolated from the others. What do you think?"

"Sure," Elizabeth replied.

Kane knew that would be her answer, but he sure wished it wasn't.

As they walked, Schafter removed a walkie-talkie from her belt and placed a call to a sergeant located elsewhere in the facility, letting him know that they were on their way and requesting that inmate Morris be prepared for their visit.

"This inmate," Schafter informed Elizabeth, "is a real puzzle. Very quiet guy, you never know what to expect from him. I know I never would've expected him to attack a guard but that's what he did the other day. Practically bit his ear off. The inmate is in here on a drug-related charge, but I didn't know he could be that violent. When an inmate assaults a guard there's a lot of resentment when he's allowed a therapy dog visit. Some of the staff thinks the prisoner is being rewarded, but it's really just an effort to calm him and maybe bring him 'round. You know, kind of like treating cruelty with kindness. Trying to break the cycle, I guess."

Elizabeth and Kane followed their escort through a complex series of hallways as Kane worried that even with his excellent sense of smell he would have great difficulty finding his way out of the complex should the need arise.

Their walk eventually led them to an elevator that delivered them to still another hallway and a secure chamber where a sliding door was opened electronically by an unseen operator only to close behind them before another door slid open to admit them to a spacious area beyond. A staff observation room with its darkened glass towered over the area against one wall flanked by doors leading to other pods. One side of the space was dominated by a glass barrier separating it from a moderately sized exercise area whose far wall contained windows from which outside light streamed. On the opposite side, where Kane and Elizabeth stood, two deputies sat at a desk located in front of a door and another glass panel behind which could be seen several small wire-mesh lockups, only large enough to hold a bed, toilet, and prisoner. The cells reminded Kane of a dog run.

Officer Schafter greeted the officer at the desk who was completing a report on a computer. A friendly conversation between them was soon interrupted by the entrance of six deputies and a sergeant through one of the connecting doors. They were accompanying a prisoner who was shackled hand and foot by chains and Elizabeth and Kane immediately recognized him. He was the individual they had encountered a few days previously at the Men's Central Jail next door who was mourning the loss of his dog. This was Morris.

He was lead to a round metal table and bench near one of the walls. Two of the deputies secured him while the sergeant and other deputies watched closely. As they went about their work, Morris looked not at Elizabeth but at Kane, who returned his attention with a slight wag of his tail. Though the huge man sat looking at him without expression, the collie sensed he had no reason to fear him. Instead, he perceived that hidden beneath his considerable bulk there existed a sensitivity and gentleness that he was at great lengths to keep hidden.

When they had finished their work, the deputies stepped back from the inmate and all but the sergeant, Schafter, Elizabeth and Kane exited the room.

Morris was securely chained to the table, but he was allowed one free hand which he used to reach out to Kane.

"Come on over here, my friend," Morris said to the dog in a quiet, gravelly voice. "I'm glad you came back to see me."

Kane stepped toward the inmate and stood at his side while Elizabeth held both hands on his leash, prepared to pull him away from danger if any should occur.

Morris softly stroked Kane's back with his unshackled hand, occasionally moaning softly to himself as if the sensation of petting the dog brought him the same pleasure he might experience if he were receiving a back rub. After a few minutes, Morris made a move forward, and the sergeant standing before him tensed in anticipation of a violent move, but he was only checking the limitations of his restraints before sliding off the bench to seat himself on the concrete floor next to Kane, who in turn laid down beside him.

Though Morris did not smile, he remained calm and relaxed as he closed his eyes and rolled his head back, thoroughly absorbing the sensation of peace and rest he was absorbing from the creature beside him.

"This is Kane," Elizabeth said to him. "He's a collie, and he's eight years old."

"Hello there, Kane," Morris said leaning his head forward and speaking very quietly into his ear. "I've never seen a real collie in person before, only on TV. I'm very pleased to make your acquaintance. I hope I didn't scare you, my friend. I'm not really a bad, bad, person. I want you to know that. I just got a little mistreated by somebody, that's all."

The sergeant and Schafter exchanged a glance that told Elizabeth they doubted the statement.

"Anyway," Morris continued speaking softly in Kane's ear, "I'm calmed down now, and it's just you and me."

As Morris continued talking, his voice dropped to a near whisper that could only be heard by the dog. While keeping a watch on the prisoner, the three people before him began talking amongst themselves, unable to hear what Morris was saying. Kane could hear every word.

"I don't know how much you can understand of what I'm saying to you," he whispered, "but I got to have somebody to talk to. I can't trust nobody around here and what I got to say ain't nobody's business anyhow. But I need somebody to listen, and I bet you're a lot like my dog, Maggie . . . ."

Morris choked up for a moment before continuing.

"That was my dog's name, the one they killed. Maggie was her name. I used to talk to her like I'm talking to you now and she always made me feel better. I could tell her secrets, and I knew she wouldn't tell nobody else."

Occasionally during Morris' talk, one of the doors from the pods would open, and staff members would pass through to the secure chamber where the electronic door would slide open to allow exit and Morris would comment on them to Kane.

111

"That officer there," he said as one passed through, "he ain't too awful bad. Pretty much sticks to business and don't give no crap to nobody that don't give it to him. But that son-of-a-bitch that kept harassing me? He laughed when he heard the cops killed my dog. Well, I don't take nothin' off nobody, you know? I did what I had to do, and I'd do it again. But then they threw me in isolation 'cause they was afraid I was some kind of mental case, and they weren't sure what I was going to do next. My lawyer says if I behave I might get out of this place pretty quick. Well, I'll try, but let me tell you, my friend . . . ."

Morris stopped in mid-sentence as two deputies moved through. They were accompanying a handcuffed prisoner who smiled as he passed. Elizabeth recognized him as the inmate Officer Vega had identified as Rodney Hawkins at the Men's Central Jail a few days ago. She felt a familiar chill return.

Kane recognized him too. A low growl formed in his throat. Morris felt the vibration in Kane's throat.

"Yeah," he whispered to the dog, "you're a pretty good judge of character, aren't you? That man right there, he's one of the worst there is. I've had some dealings with him on the outside and you believe me when I say you want to stay clear of him. He got arrested on a murder rap, but I hear they're gonna let his sorry ass go. Can you believe that?"

Hawkins and the deputies accompanying him had paused at the entrance to the security chamber waiting for the automated door to be released by the guard in the security tower.

"He's got to have some kind of help pretty high up, I'll tell you that," Morris continued. "I also got it on pretty good authority that he's getting out so he can pull off a contract job on somebody to keep 'em from testifying against him in court.

112

Yeah. 'Course nobody in here would believe me, even if I tried to tell them. Then some of his gangsters would come after me. My life wouldn't be worth shit."

Still waiting for the door to be opened, Hawkins perused the area. It may have been when his icy gaze settled on Elizabeth, it may have been Morris' next words, but it was probably the combination that prompted Kane next action.

"Can you believe it? He's gonna get outta here and go do a hit job on the only witness who saw him commit murder."

With that, Kane suddenly and unexpectedly lunged away, breaking free of Morris and yanking the other end of the leash out of Elizabeth's hands as he headed toward Hawkins, barking fiercely. Elizabeth screamed after him, and he reached Hawkins and his deputies at the exact moment the door slid open, allowing them to enter the security chamber. As he stood before the door barking, Elizabeth retrieved the end of the leash and pulled him back.

"Kane!" she shouted at the dog, jerking on the leash. "What's gotten into you? You've never done this before! Stop it!"

He stopped barking as the door began to slide shut in front of him. Hawkins stood facing them without moving, the disquieting smile on his face unchanged, until the door was completely closed and he was led out of the chamber on the opposite side.

Schafter joined Elizabeth while Kane remained rigid and defiant.

"Don't you reprimand that dog!" Morris called out to Elizabeth. "That man ain't no good, I tell ya. Kane knows what he's doing!"

"I think that'll do it for today's visit," the sergeant said as he summoned his deputies on his walkie-talkie to assist him in escorting Morris back to his cell.

"I don't know what that was all about," Elizabeth said to Schafter. "I am so sorry. That was totally unacceptable. I don't know what to say."

"Well," Schafter said with a smile, "I suppose even Kane has his standards. He must not have liked the way that guy was looking at you."

A muted growl still rumbled in Kane's throat. The way the man had looked at Elizabeth was not the only reason for his frenzy. He resolved not to keep his anger in check should he meet the man again.

CHAPTER SIXTEEN

Elizabeth and Kane were halfway out the door of the house late in the afternoon after her jail visit when her cell phone rang. It was Rob.

"Did I catch you at a bad time?" he asked.

"Oh, no," she assured him, trying not to come across too delighted at the sound of his voice, at least not this early in their relationship. "I was just on my way out the door to drop Kane off at Pauline's place. She said Becky had a rough night last night so we thought we'd let Kane stay over. What's up?"

"Nothing special. I mean, well, I don't mean it's not special but . . . ." He stumbled over his words. Elizabeth could picture a blush on his face. "What I mean to say is, you have time for a coffee?"

"Now?" she asked, glancing at her watch. "Let's see, I promised my mom I'd have dinner with her and Ben tonight. Sure. I should have time. I could go for a good, tall frappe or frappucino, or whatever they call those things."

"Great!" he exclaimed. "You want to drop Kane off first or . . . ."

May was looking around the kitchen doorway from her seat in front of the computer. The expression on her face silently asked who was on the phone. Elizabeth stepped out the front door for privacy.

"No, that's okay," she said to Rob. "Are you nearby?"

"Yeah, I am," he replied. "I could just . . . ."

"Good. There's a Starbucks on Imperial by the freeway. Why don't we meet there? I can drop Kane off afterward."

"I know that place," Rob confirmed. "See you there."

The front door opened enough for May to peek her face through.

"Got a date?" she asked with a teasing smile.

"No!" Elizabeth replied with a scowl.

"'The lady doth protest too much, methinks'," her mother said.

"Oh, Mom, please," Elizabeth said, as she headed to her car. "We're just going for coffee. Come on, Kane."

"Coffee?" her mother laughingly called after her. "Is that what the're calling it these days?"

Elizabeth chose to ignore her, opening her car door for Kane.

"Kane," May called after him, "Keep an eye on her!"

Elizabeth started her car and guided it back out of the driveway.

Kane understood what teasing was all about. He'd even enjoyed his share of it, but he didn't always recognize it when humans did it. Like now. They were going to meet a cop. Why should he have to keep an eye on Elizabeth?

At the coffee shop, Elizabeth and Kane found a shaded table on the patio while Rob went inside to place their order. He returned a short while later balancing a coffee for himself and a blended beverage for Elizabeth. He didn't forget Kane, placing a paper bowl full of water under the table for him.

"So, Becky had a bad night?" he asked with concern, pulling up a chair.

"That's what I hear," Elizabeth answered. "Pauline has an appointment with a child therapist coming up."

"She probably can't get her there fast enough," Rob said with a frown. "I worry about her."

Elizabeth smiled. "Do you always become this emotionally involved with the victims you encounter in your job?"

"Oh," he replied, "I've been accused of getting too personally involved sometimes. Maybe this one has my stomach in knots because her dad was an old friend. Or maybe . . . I don't know."

Elizabeth got the impression there was something more to his concern.

"What made you become a cop, anyway?" she asked.

"I guess it started with my brother," he began.

"He persuaded you?"

"He was killed by a hit-and-run driver when he was six. I was twelve. I was his big brother. He looked up to me. My old man was a lout. My mother was an alcoholic. I'd wtached out for him his whole life and I was his protector and I failed him. I was goofing off with my friends and I should have been holding his hand when he crossed that street. I vowed I'd catch the guy driving that car and hold him accountable. I never did, but I guess that's what prompted me to become a cop. I'm still looking for that guy."

The conversation had taken an unexpected turn. Elizabeth could see that Rob was struggling with an internal demon and she instinctively reached across the table for his hand but he pulled it away.

"You were still just a kid," she said sympathetically. "You can't blame yourself for what happened."

"I'm sorry," he interrupted. "I'd really rather not talk about it."

Elizabeth decided not to press it and the two of them sat sipping their drinks in

silence for a moment.

"Funny," he said after a while. "I hardly know you, and I'm sitting here telling you my life story. I don't usually pour on the melodrama this quick with somebody I just met."

"Well," she said, trying to brighten things up, "Becky's lucky to have you looking out for her."

"Yeah, well, I'm not off to a very good start," he sighed. "My chief found out about me nosing around into Zach's case and I got put on suspension."

"Oh no," Elizabeth responded with concern.

"I'm not quitting," he said firmly. "Whatever Zach was looking into must have been something big and I owe it to him to pick up where he left off."

"Oh, Rob," Elizabeth said, reaching for his hand again. "Be careful. Zach got himself killed. You could be in a lot of danger."

"So could Becky," he shot back. "I'll be careful, but I'm not going to leave her unprotected."

Kane liked the sound of that.

CHAPTER SEVENTEEN

It may have been Becky's mother's words at the funeral that day, "*I'm afraid for Becky!*" It may have been the girl's fearful reaction to the stranger who had visited her home a couple of nights ago or the warning James Morris had given. It may have been a keen awareness of potential danger hard-wired into collies since the days they protected their flock from wolves. From wherever it originated, an internal alarm wakened Kane as he lay beside Becky while she slept.

All of his senses immediately energized, he lay frozen, tuned in to every sound, every smell, every shadow in the darkened room.

Kane's evening with Becky and her mother had been bright and fun and uneventful, but now, in the middle of night, there was darkness. Now there was danger.

The sky was overcast but a faint light from the street was filtered by the shuttered window, casting shadows across the bed, and an inconsistent wind delivered the sound of rustling leaves and a distant siren.

Assuring that Becky was still asleep, Kane stepped down from the bed and looked out the window. Through the partially closed blinds, he could see no movement outside, but he knew that sometimes there could be danger in what is not seen.

Not satisfied with all he had observed, he left the room and peered into the dimness of the front room, where only a small red light on the television burned steadily. All was still, and though everything was in its proper place, the darkness rendered every object sinister.

Pushing aside a partially closed door, Kane examined Pauline's room. A dim green light from her clock radio fell across her face, in repose, the heavy breath of sleep the only sound he heard.

Glancing in the bathroom, he moved next to the kitchen where he paused in the doorway to make his evaluation. Nothing, save the soft hum of the refrigerator. A glass paneled door stood at the back of the kitchen, and the fur on Kane's neck suddenly stood up as a shadow quickly passed by, momentarily blocking the feeble light outside. He resisted the impulse to bark, for fear he might frighten Pauline and Becky before he could positively identify what lurked out there.

Rushing to the door, Kane surveyed the modest back patio but he was not fast enough to catch the shadow, and he saw only a small, portable, barbecue next to an outdoor metal table and two chairs. A leaf moved slowly across the concrete floor, pushed along by a slight wind.

Had it been a cat? A rat?

Sniffing along the bottom of the door, he identified the source of his fear, and in a flash, he bolted for Becky's room.

There, framed in silhouette behind the shutters, stood a tall, smiling phantom looking down at the sleeping figure on the bed.

Kane ran to the window, barking wildly, and the shadowy spectre disappeared. Becky sat bolt upright, her eyes blinking, and Pauline rushed in, flipping on the light.

"Kane!" Pauline shouted at him, not totally awake yet. "What on earth . . . ?"

He continued to bark, then ran frantically to the front door where he darted about in a plea to be let outside.

"Do you have to pee?" Pauline wondered. "If that's all you wanted . . . ."

When Kane continued his frenzy, Elizabeth ran to her room and returned with a slip-leash in her hand, sliding into a bathrobe.

"What's wrong, Mommy?" Becky wondered as she joined them.

"Stay here," Pauline instructed as she placed the noose of the leash around Kane's neck. "I'm just taking him out to potty. We'll be right back."

The moment the door was opened, Kane bolted with such energy, the leash was yanked from Pauline's hand. After running to the center of the small yard, he rushed to the shrubs that separated Pauline's apartment from the apartment next door.

As he frantically darted about, sniffing for clues, Pauline retrieved his leash.

"Kane," she said tugging at him, "this is ridiculous! Come on back in the house before the landlord finds out you're here."

The dog suddenly stopped and cocked his head. From a distance, he could hear a vehicle engine as it was started and driven away. The monster was gone.

As Pauline pulled Kane into the house, she was met by Becky.

"What's wrong with Kane, Mommy?" the girl asked.

"It sure beats me, honey," her mother replied, removing Kane's leash. "Let's get back to bed."

After tucking Becky in, Pauline paused at the doorway before turning out the light. Kane's behavior made her uneasy, but she hoped he had merely been alarmed by something blown by the wind. She clung to that thought.

But Kane was certain of what he had seen. Morris had warned him.

He remained awake throughout the rest of the night.

CHAPTER EIGHTEEN

Rob Martinez leaned against his car, checking his phone for messages as he waited for his friend Danny Ralston to arrive. Danny had some information about the Burton case that was too important to bury, asking him to meet him that evening at the murder scene.

"And Rob," Danny whispered, "make sure you're not followed."

Rob didn't need to be told. After talking with the store's owner earlier that day, he was sure things were going to get uglier.

"Why wasn't your surveillance camera working that night?" Rob asked, pointing to the camera that was mounted on the ceiling above the door.

"Who said it wasn't working?" the store owner asked.

"Where's the recording?" Rob inquired.

"I gave it to that cop. Only copy I had," the owner said. "Only camera installed in here. Only one workin' anyway. The one behind the counter needs to be fixed. I been meanin' to put another one in. Guess I better do that."

"Do you remember the cop's name?" Rob asked.

"Nope. Some guy, balding, dressed in a pretty nifty suit for a cop. Showed me his badge and all. Say, why don't you know all this already?"

The store owner's eyes narrowed.

"You sure you're a cop? Wait a minute. Where's your badge?" he said.

Rob thanked him for his time and made a swift exit.

Now, as he sipped coffee from a paper cup, he wondered what his next move should be. Maybe Danny would have the answer.

A short while later, a grey sedan pulled into the cul-de-sac and parked behind Rob's car. Danny turned off his headlights and engine. He made sure they were alone before he got out. He lit a cigarette, nodding a greeting as he stood next to Rob.

"Trouble sleeping?" Rob asked. "You look like hell."

"What are you talking about?" Danny answered, taken aback. "I don't look any worse than I normally . . . ."

He stopped in mid-sentence, realizing his leg was being pulled and he waved his friend away. With a smirk, he took a long pull on his cigarette, held it, then blew it through his nose.

"Well, I gotta admit," Danny said with a frown, "the more I looked into this, the more I find don't add up. I don't know . . . I mean, like his cell phone. We never found it, but we did get our hands on his phone records. Listen to this, the day Zach died, he placed a call to Takimoto's office, but when Mosher asked the captain about it, he said he never got any call from Zach that day. So he asks his secretary if he fielded any calls from him, but the guy gets real antsy all of a sudden. Says he has no recollection, has no record of it."

"I know that guy. Glasser." Rob said, recalling the strange way he had watched him when he visited the captain a few days previously. "Very efficient."

"Normally, yeah. So Mosher shows him the phone records. Now all of a sudden Glasser remembers. Starts apologizing. Says Zach wanted to talk to the captain but when Glasser told him he was busy, Zach said he'd call back and hung up."

"Pretty odd, uh?"

"Pfft!" Danny replied sarcastically. "A shiny new Lexus in Simmon's parking space? What do you think?"

"Well, let's see," Rob pondered. "Zach was investigating drug rings. Sounds like some of our boys are on the take, starting with Glasser."

"Mosher figures Zach had all his facts together and he was trying to set up a meeting with Takimoto's office to spill the beans and name some names. The captain was the only one he trusted down there. We figure Glasser fielded the call and let *somebody* know about it. *Somebody* silenced Zach with a bullet."

"Hawkins," Rob said with a nod. "Mosher locked him up."

"Yeah, well here's the thing," Danny said, slowly exhaling a puff of smoke. "Hawkins got released. No charges."

"What?"

"In Mosher's eagerness to lock up Hawkins, he rushed him at his place and found the murder weapon, but somehow somebody on the team forgot to get a search warrant. The evidence is inadmissible."

"I thought I heard Mosher is a pretty thorough detective. How could he forget something like that?"

"He thought it was taken care of, but somehow the request was held up on somebody's desk somewhere, and it hadn't been approved when Mosher and his team went in."

"You sure Mosher's not in on it himself?" Rob asked suspiciously, squinting his eyes.

Danny shook his head. "I tell you that guy is honest as the day is long. He's just a big brown-noser, that's all. Too eager to please the boys at the top, and I mean all the boys up to the mayor. But he screwed up on this one, and now he's mad as hell. That's why he's scrutinizing the case more closely now. He's gotta vindicate himself."

Rob told Danny about the missing surveillance recording and the mysterious cop who confiscated it. Danny dropped his cigarette and crushed it with his heel.

"You know," he said, "if Zach was going to meet with the captain, he must have had some evidence to turn over to him. He wouldn't have gone in there empty-handed. He's got to have hidden some notes somewhere, some pictures, *something*. We never found a damn thing. Where the hell would he have hidden it?"

"Funny thing is," Rob said with a chuckle, "I bet I know a dog that could sniff it out. He's almost smart enough to do it."

"Ain't no dog that smart," Danny said, shaking his head. "He understand English?"

Rob nodded his head in agreement over the absurdity of the idea.

"Are they keeping Hawkins under surveillance?" he asked.

"I don't know what good that'll do," Danny scoffed. "Who knows how many are on the take on this thing? What we need to do is find out who the liaison is between the authorities and the top man with the money that's giving cars away. That's the guy we need."

A car drove by slowly at the mouth of the cul de sac, its lights on high beam. Danny nervously lit another cigarette.

"I gotta go," he said. "I'll keep you posted. And Rob, watch out. You could wind up like Zach. Don't forget that.

And keep an eye on your friends, especially that little girl. Could be nobody you know is safe. Not even your dog friend."

CHAPTER NINETEEN

On a scorching morning on a typically uncloudy day in late August as heat records were being broken throughout the Southern California area, Rob Martinez parked his car next to the curb in front of Pauline and Becky's apartment.

Elizabeth was seated next to Rob in the front seat while Ben and Kane sat in the back. She was cautiously cheerful that on this day that they had planned a brief hike and picnic in the San Gabriel Mountains, her brother appeared to be feeling unusually vigorous. Perhaps he was buoyed by the prospect of the adventure ahead of them.

Though May had at first protested against her son participating in such an outing, she realized that the mountain air might be good for him if he was up to it, and when Ben himself demanded to go, she relented. May had watched him sit listlessly for weeks as he silently endured the sickening treatments he was forced to undergo. Treatment was being withheld for a week to allow him to regain some strength, and during that time some color had returned to his cheeks, and he even found enough energy to play with Kane in the backyard.

Watching the two of them explore the small yard cheered May for the first time in a couple of months and she even laughed to herself as she watched Kane frolic, his spirits high, as he ran about in circles around Ben. She reflected on the thought that Kane had likely been as depressed as she had been and she suspected that depression might have been what provoked the display of anger at the jail that Elizabeth had related to her.

May was doubtful when Rob assured her he would see to it that Ben would not become overly exhausted. But, though she had known him for a short time, Rob had won her trust, and she finally accepted his promise to be careful.

Becky had been watching from her first story apartment window, and as soon as she spotted Rob's car, she came rushing out to the curb to meet her friends. Her mother followed, carrying a small backpack she had filled with bottles of water. The backseat window near the curb had been rolled down, and Kane leaped from it to greet his friend, cheerfully barking as Becky squealed with delight.

Rob came around from his side of the car and opened the back door to admit her.

"Are you sure you can't go with us?" he asked Pauline with a smile, taking the backpack from her.

"Wish I could," she answered with a shake of her head. "I've got to go into work and play catch-up."

"Well, we'll do it again sometime," Rob said. "Maybe on a cooler day."

"There's several bottles of water in the backpack," Pauline said. "Feel free to help yourself."

"Thanks," Rob replied with a wink. "I packed quite a few extra bottles myself. Listen, I don't think we'll be up there too long. I don't want to wear Ben out, especially in this heat. I'll give you a call before we get back."

Wishing her a good day, Rob returned to the driver's side of his car and Becky and Elizabeth waved a joyful goodbye to Pauline as the car pulled away from the curb.

She waved back at them then followed the pathway back to her apartment door. She failed to notice the black Lincoln Navigator that was parked across the street a few doors down.

Now it slowly pulled into the road and made a U-turn to follow Rob's car.

Rob and his companions spent the nearly hour-long drive to their destination, singing, laughing, and telling stale jokes as they passed around a package of pretzels. Kane joined in the fun, accentuating the merriment with a bark now and then, much to the delight of Becky and Ben, who shared their pretzels with him. Elizabeth smiled as she noted her brother participating in the festivities and Kane hadn't been this happy since leaving the family vineyards.

The heat of the day had not yet reached its peak as their car pulled into a marked parking place near the small ranger's station near the head of the trail they would be hiking. As it was an early weekday morning, there weren't many other vehicles in the lot, which pleased Rob, who figured they'd pretty much have the place to themselves.

As they piled from the car, Elizabeth slipped a collar around Kane's neck and attached a leash as Becky protested.

"I know he doesn't need it," Elizabeth told her, "but we have to follow the rules. Dogs are only allowed on the trail if they're on leash."

Kane endured the humiliation with dignity. He was used to it, and he knew Elizabeth would likely divest him of it at the earliest opportunity. He understood the reason for the rule, but he was always baffled by the number of strangers he and Elizabeth encountered on their walks who would allow their leashed dog to rush toward him without first asking permission, leaving Kane to wonder what the handler thought was the purpose of the leash.

"It's okay," they would always say. "My dog is friendly. He won't bite."

Kane always enjoyed Elizabeth's typical response to that remark, "How do you know *my* dog won't bite?"

Playing along with the tease, Kane would assume a menacing stare into the stranger's face, whose expression would quickly change from a smile to one of uncertainty as the obnoxious dog was pulled away. However, on the rare occasion when the offending canine was an un-spayed female, Kane was inclined to assume a much friendlier demeanor.

As Rob and the kids gathered their backpacks from the car, Kane treated himself to a vigorous shake and then led Elizabeth to a nearby post which he sniffed before confirming it met the standard he set for the lifting of his leg. Giving the post a final, approving sniff, he turned to rejoin the group, Elizabeth still at the opposite end of his leash.

It was at that moment that Kane eyed the black SUV that slowly turned into the fenced parking lot. It paused a few moments at the entrance before selecting a parking stall nearest the lot entryway, rather than choosing one of the many available spaces closer to the starting point of the trail. Kane could barely make out the silouhette of the driver through the heavily tinted windows, but he didn't like the way he seemed to be watching them as he remained in his parking space with the engine still running. He liked less a distinct aroma he isolated from the many other smells his nose was picking up. Kane started to move slowly and cautiously toward the curious vehicle, but as Rob and the kids headed toward the hiking trail, Elizabeth pulled him back to join them, and Kane did his best to keep the SUV in sight. He watched it over his shoulder for as long as he could until the dirt trail they were hiking made a turn into a wooded area, blocking it from his view.

"Kane, come on, boy," Elizabeth told him as she gave his leash a slight tug.

Though he responded to her command, his movement was sluggish. The forest through which they traveled was thick and the brush dense, which added to Kane's unease and during their walk he frequently stopped to lift his nose into the air, attempting to discern the distance between them and the host of the ominous smell that followed them.

"I wonder what's gotten into him," she remarked to Rob. "He's been acting so strange ever since he went after that inmate the other day. Today, on the way over here, he was happier than I've seen him since Ben started his treatments, but now look at him. Something's spooked him."

Rob studied the dog as they walked.

"Well, there's not any mystery over the way he reacted at Twin Towers," he told her. "He must have known who Hawkins was. I think he can be forgiven for a little animosity there."

"I guess," she replied, "but he normally wouldn't act like that toward someone who wasn't posing an immediate threat. Fortunately, the Twin Towers staff understood. They agreed to let him come back, but Claire thinks it would be best if we keep him away from there for a while."

Rob took note of Kane's distraction as the dog walked cautiously, not at Elizabeth's side as he usually did, but reluctantly behind her as he continued to glance over his shoulder. Maybe someone was following them. Rob didn't want to make anyone uneasy, but Kane knew something.

Kane understood their conversation, but their lack of concern over the possibility that they might be followed made him feel responsible for their safety and prevented him from enjoying what for him would have been a joyous occasion. A walk in the woods would generally flood his mind with wonderful memories of the life he enjoyed before he came to live with the McLaughlins, but now he had a responsibility to remain vigilant. It was a duty willingly accepted by his breed many years ago in the hills of Scotland when collies were relied upon to keep watch over their flock of sheep and to keep them together and protected them from harm. That duty was genetically ingrained, and in the absence of sheep, it was now transferred to his companions, just as it had been during his overnight stay with Becky.

When Ben and Becky bounded a bit ahead of the group, Kane would run after them, prompting Elizabeth to temporarily remove his leash, allowing him to catch up. Then he rushed before them and attempted to herd them back to rejoin the "flock." It wasn't a wolf Kane sensed nearby. It was a predator far more dangerous.

It wasn't long before Ben's energy was spent and soon Rob and Elizabeth found him seated on a rock beside the trail, Becky beside him and Kane pacing nervously in front of him.

"Whoa!" Rob exclaimed. "Looks like someone could use a lift."

Elizabeth asked Ben how he felt as Rob opened a bottle of water and handed it to him. Ben didn't respond as he quickly drained the bottle and attempted to stand but his eagerness was not a match for his lack of strength, and he promptly collapsed back on his seat.

"Okay then," Rob said. He handed off his backpack to Elizabeth and then turned to kneel in front of him, exposing his back for Ben to mount. "All aboard and off we go."

Reluctant at first, Ben allowed Rob, with Elizabeth's help, to lift him, piggy-back style onto his back. Rob gave no sign that Ben was a burden as he cheerfully shifted him to a comfortable position before vigorously resuming their hike. Elizabeth and Becky joined hands and followed close behind, and Kane, free from his leash, at first followed them but then suddenly stopped.

The dog could hear the sound of footsteps approaching from the trail behind them. The serpentine route of the path made it impossible for him to see who was following and he wasn't certain from this distance if the footsteps and the ominous smell he discerned in the parking lot belonged to the same individual. He braced himself and stood in the middle of the path, ready to meet the creature who was gradually approaching, then gathered himself as he prepared to leap upon it the instant it came into view.

Through small breaks in the tangled leaves, he could see movement as the stranger came nearer. Kane could make out that it was a single individual but whether friend or foe he could not yet identify.

Suddenly Elizabeth's voice rang out from the path behind him as she called Kane's name, coinciding with the exact moment the stranger rounded the corner. A young bearded man, dressed in shorts and aided by a hiking stick appeared before him and quickly jumped back, startled by the vision of the dog who seemed to be ready to leap upon him.

Kane relaxed as the man raised his walking stick in defense, his eyes wide with fear. The man's smell and physical appearance told the dog this was not the menace he had feared it might be and he turned and raced up the path to rejoin his comrades as the hiker watched him go.

Gentle Hero

Before long, Kane caught up with his group and Elizabeth chided him for falling behind. He paid little attention to her words but paused once more to sniff the air behind them. The smell of the lone hiker was receding.

But there was that other smell, and it was becoming stronger. Over the next thirty minutes, Kane remained wary, doing his best to keep track of the location of the stalker who seemed to move from the trail into the woods beside it and then back again, as if searching for a satisfactory spot to remain concealed. A few fellow hikers passed from the path before them, making their way back to the trail's starting point.

"There it is! This is the spot I wanted to show you," Rob shouted as they neared a stream of water that flowed through a wide opening in the forest to join the trail, gurgling and splashing, twisting and winding itself alongside.

They found a clearing beside the path which afforded them a convenient spot to lay out their picnic lunch. Kane stood nearby, nervously watching for movement in the thicket. Rob gently lowered Ben to the ground as Elizabeth fished a blanket out of her backpack and spread it on a level spot surrounded by several rocks that conveniently provided seating. Becky removed her shoes and socks and sat at the edge of the stream, splashing her feet in the water while Ben stood, transfixed by a small waterfall upstream where the water dropped from an overhanging stone. He watched as it splashed to the pond four feet below before it traveled downstream.

"How did you know about this place?" Elizabeth asked Rob as he helped her set out the picnic feast.

"Actually, he replied, " I wasn't sure I'd find this spot again. I haven't been here since I was a kid, I used to hike up here with my brother and my mom when she . . . when she

136

was sober. The place hasn't hasn't changed much. We had some great times up here before . . . ."

Elizabeth wanted to talk to him about his brother, but since it seemed to be a topic that was off limits to him, she hoped he might open up more when they became better friends.

"What's he doing?" Rob wondered with a chuckle as he pointed toward the stream.

Ben had removed his shoes and was standing in the stream, holding his head under the small waterfall, occasionally stopping to catch his breath before putting his head back under. Becky giggled.

"Ben?" Elizabeth called to him.

After a moment, he looked up at her from where he stood, pointing to the waterfall.

"The back side of water," he said before putting his head back under.

Elizabeth laughed at his observation but wondered from where it had sprung.

After a moment, seeing that his sister didn't seem to understand, Ben tried to clarify.

"Schweitzer Falls," he reminded her. "The back side of water!"

Racking her brain, she finally understood his reference.

"Oh, that's right!" she chuckled.

"What's he talking about?" Becky asked.

"Well," Elizabeth explained, "When I first got down here from school, he and Mom and I went to Disneyland. Have you ever been on the Jungle Cruise ride there?"

"Sure, lots of times," Becky replied. "The guy who drives the boat says lots of silly things. Sometimes it's a woman."

"That's right," Elizabeth agreed. "and at one point the boat goes behind a big waterfall and the captain of the boat says, 'Look! The back side of water!' It really impressed Ben, and he made us keep taking him back on the ride all day so he could see the 'back side of water' again. It was so funny. We laughed so hard. Wait 'til I tell Mom about this. Becky, don't you try that. Your mom might not like you getting your hair wet."

They all watched Ben in silence for a while as he studied the waterfall. Everyone, that is, except Kane, whose attention was directed toward the high shrubbery among the tree trunks on the opposite side of the stream. All of his senses told him that the danger he feared was slowly approaching from that area and was growing nearer. He stood frozen, his tail tucked and his ears back as a low growl formed in his throat.

"Okay, let's eat, " Elizabeth called out as she and Rob finished setting out their small lunch.

Becky quickly joined them, finding a suitable rock on which to sit and Ben soon followed, shaking water from his head.

As Elizabeth handed the children a sandwich, a bottle of water and a small bag of chips, Rob noticed Kane's peculiar posture.

"What's that all about?" he asked Elizabeth as he nodded in the dog's direction.

Elizabeth looked up, and a disquieting feeling of unease crept over her. She knew Kane did not react with false alarm.

"Maybe there's a mailman out there," Rob said to the children with a smile. "Or maybe . . . maybe it's a bear!"

Ben made a frightened sound and reached for Elizabeth, holding her tight. Becky gasped.

"Rob. Please!" Elizabeth scolded him. "Don't scare the kids."

Rob was immediately remorseful. "Oh, I'm sorry. Seriously, I'm sure there aren't any bears around this area. The rangers keep them pretty well monitored."

Ben began to whine softly as he watched Kane, and Elizabeth held him firmly and spoke to him with soft, comforting words. Becky ran to her, grabbing her arm and holding it tight.

"I'm afraid of bears!" Becky declared, her eyes wide.

Noticing the children's anxiety, Kane rushed to Ben and gave him a lick on the cheek before turning to Becky and doing the same.

"There, you see?" Elizabeth said to them. "Kane is here to protect you. Both of you."

Kane was now aware that the creature in the woods had come to a stop. They were being watched. Nervously, the collie moved to Becky and stood in front of her. Morris' warning and Pauline's fear echoed in his mind again. He was certain the figure he had seen at Becky's window had returned.

Rob shared Kane's unease.

"Kane," he said, hoping to cheer Elizabeth and the children, "haven't you ever seen a rabbit?"

"A rabbit?" Becky asked, peering into the brush.

"Sure," Rob said. "Didn't you see it?"

"I don't see any rabbit," Elizabeth responded, squinting her eyes.

Kane didn't either. But he did hear a clicking sound. He didn't know what it was, but he didn't like it and he had enough. Lunging into the water and bounding onto the opposite side, it took him only three long, swift, strides to reach the brush and, with incredible speed, he bolted into the thick bushes and disappeared from view.

"Kane!" Elizabeth shouted after him.

"Wait here," Rob ordered her before following Kane across the river.

He found that penetrating the bushes was not as easy as the dog had made it appear but he eventually made his way through the brush and was soon running amid the shrubbery and trees in pursuit. Though he couldn't see Kane, several tree branches ahead of Rob still swayed, having been pushed aside, a sure sign he was on the right path. Calling after Kane, Rob fought back tree limbs and bushes as he attempted to catch up, but he was no match for the collie's speed and ability.

Kane's sense of hearing and smell told him that he might be closing in on his target as he bravely pushed forward through the bushes, heedless of the obstacles in his path as he brushed them aside or leaped over them with equal ease. He might just as well have been pursuing a wolf, and a thrill of exhilaration instinctively took hold and a single purpose of mind dominated as he anticipated overtaking the beast.

Suddenly, he stopped.

The creature ahead of him was no longer running, and Kane could barely make out the tall, dark-skinned man some distance ahead. He was peering around a tree in his direction. Kane recognized the scent and the smile on the face of Rodney Hawkins. He could hear that the man was breathing heavily and it was evident that he was waiting for his pursuer to come closer. Kane sensed a trap, and he was ready when Hawkins stepped from behind the tree, holding a handgun with both hands as he aimed it in his direction. With lightning speed, Kane jumped amid a growth of shrubbery beside him, narrowly avoiding a bullet, the loud crack of the pistol echoing amid the surrounding trees.

Some distance behind, Rob stopped, recognizing the sound of gunfire.

"Kane!" he shouted. "Stay down! I'm on my way!"

He had called out instinctively, giving no thought as to whether Kane understood, but by yelling he hoped he would scare off whoever fired the shot. With renewed effort, Rob pushed his way through the bushes toward the sound of the gunshot. He wished he still had his weapon.

Having heard Rob's voice, Hawkins, hiding behind the tree ahead of Kane, turned and continued running. Kane would have none of it. He continued his pursuit, now keeping in mind that the beast in front of him was capable of turning on him at any moment with lethal force. Kane had once observed a hunter in the woods near his home use a rifle to kill a deer, so he understood the power of the instrument. It gave him no pause.

Dodging and swerving through the forest growth, Hawkins eventually reached the clearing where the parking lot was located and ran with breakneck speed to his vehicle. He reached in his pocket for the key fob remote, unlocked the door and threw himself behind the steering wheel before slamming the door shut.

With a squeal of rubber, Hawkins shifted into reverse, backed out of the parking space and turned to escape through the lot entrance. Kane, kept pace with it, barking wildly. Hawkins slammed the accelerator to the floor and swerved slightly into him just enough to graze him with the front bumper. The dog was knocked off his feet but had the presence of mind to roll out of the way as the SUV sped past him.

Rob caught only a brief glimpse of the vehicle as he finally made his way out of the forest edge.

Kane slowly stood and shook himself. His hip was sore but didn't prevent him from walking, albeit with a slight limp. As Rob raced to his side and knelt beside him, the collie held his gaze in the direction Hawkins had just escaped.

"Who in the hell was that guy?" Rob wondered aloud.

Kane knew, and he was the only one who did. He wished he could tell Rob, but since he couldn't, he was Becky's only hope.

CHAPTER TWENTY

After reuniting with Elizabeth and the children, Rob explained to them what had occurred, and together they reported the incident to the park ranger's office. The ranger in charge accepted the report with due concern, but Rob agreed with him that there wasn't a great deal anyone could do at this point. The mysterious individual was long gone and there were no cameras in the area that might identify him. The best the ranger could promise to do was share the information with the local police and other officials in the area. Rob thanked him for his help and led his friends back to his car.

"It was probably just some idiot out on a hike with his gun is all," Rob told them on the drive home. "Kane must have scared him, and he defended himself."

"You think so?" Elizabeth asked, wanting to believe him.

"Sure."

"Really?"

Silence.

"No. No, I don't," he said softly.

More silence.

"What should we do?"

Rob didn't have an answer.

Ben remained physically exhausted by the demand the hike had placed upon him and by the anxiety which had overtaken him when Kane had rushed into the woods.

Becky was visibly distressed. Since the night she witnessed the death of her father, it took very little to frighten her, and the sound of the gunshot fired in the woods had thrown her into a panic. It was only with extreme effort that Elizabeth was able to calm and console her. Sitting in the backseat of Rob's car, Becky clutched Kane closely, both arms embracing him tightly as the car wound its way down from the mountains.

Kane could feel her trembling as she held him close. He ignored the ache in his hip, worrying instead about her safety and wondering when and how the phantom might strike next.

The wind was gaining strength as Rob parked his car in front of May's house. He

had called ahead to relate their experience to the children's mothers and Pauline was with May to meet them as they walked up the pathway. Rushing to the car, she flung wide the door and embraced her daughter, whispering words of comfort. May invited them all into the house and Kane kept close to Pauline as she carried Becky inside.

Assembling in the front room, Elizabeth told them the details of their encounter as May and Pauline fussed over their children. Ben pulled away from his mother and checked Kane's water bowl before pouring kibble into his food dish. Kane gratefully devoured his meal while the adults talked.

When the story had been told, May noticed the concern on Pauline's face.

"How about everyone stick around for dinner?" May asked cheerfully.

"Sounds good," Elizabeth responded.

"I've got a good recipe for spaghetti sauce and plenty of meat to add to the mix," May told them.

"You mean that jar we picked up yesterday at the market?" Elizabeth asked.

"There you go," May said, casting a fake frown in her daughter's direction, "giving away my secret family recipe."

"We'd love to stay," Pauline replied, smiling.

"You know," Rob said, "my experience with dinner preparation usually consists of searching through my drawer of fast-food coupons, but I'll take charge of the after-dinner cleanup if you'll allow me."

"Okay," May replied with a laugh, "but your paycheck will be docked for any dishes you break. Meantime, you're in charge of entertaining the kids."

"Now there's an assignment I'll gladly accept," he answered, and Elizabeth joined her mother and Pauline as they headed for the kitchen.

Kane moved closer to Becky as soon as her mother had left her side.

"Relax, Kane," Rob said as he patted him. "We're out of danger now, old pal." He thought for a moment before adding, "I hope."

Kane knew that wasn't true.

"Show me your gun," Ben suddenly spoke up.

"That nasty thing?" Rob answered. "Sorry pal, I don't happen to have it on me just now. See, I have to have one to do my job, but it's not something I like to show off."

"Did you ever have to shoot somebody?" Ben asked.

Kane felt Becky stiffen at the question. Rob noticed her reaction as well.

"No," he replied, then quickly attempted to change the subject. "Say, you got any games? Any sports equipment maybe?"

Ben didn't respond, and in the silence, Rob tried to think of a way to distract the kids when a tennis ball suddenly landed in the middle of the living room floor.

"I think he got a good rest on the way home," Elizabeth said to Rob from the kitchen doorway. "Sometimes he'll throw the ball to Kane, sometimes he'd rather just sit and watch somebody else do it. See what he's in the mood for today. It's been a while since he felt well enough to play."

"Excellent!" Rob exclaimed, grabbing the ball. "What do you say, guys? And what about you, Kane? You up for a game of fetch?"

Kane showed no sign of enthusiasm about the game. Unlike many dogs, he was never too keen on sports, and when it came to fetching, he could never quite grasp the concept. If the ball needed to be returned, why was it tossed away in the first place? Nevertheless, he stood and followed them through the kitchen to the back door. If the kids wanted to play the game, he was always up for a frolic with them.

"Okay, Kane's leading the way. Let's go do it then!" Rob said, giving the ball a couple of bounces.

"No bouncing balls inside the house," May shouted out from the kitchen. "Ben, tell Rob the rule."

Rob reacted to her scolding with mock pain, then motioned for Ben and Becky to join him. Slowly the two children stood and followed Kane into the backyard. He remained glued to Becky.

The backyard consisted of a modest patio with a patch of grass, surrounded by a six-foot wooden fence. A latched wooden gate that led to the front of the house rattled as the wind blew against it.

"OK," Rob said, as he placed the two children side-by-side at one end of the yard. "It's gonna be you two against Kane and me. Go ahead, Becky. You first. Throw the ball to either him or me. Let's see who drops the ball first. Go for it, Becky."

Tossing the ball gently to her, Rob backed away, preparing for his catch. Becky, however, couldn't wait. She threw him a hard ball and Rob was lucky he saw it in time to duck. It bounced off the fence behind him.

"Hey!" Rob yelled. "What was that?"

"Sorry," Becky said sheepishly.

"The object of the game is *not* to hit me in the head," Rob admonished her.

"I said I was sorry," she said, her eyes fixed on her shoes. She really was sorry now.

"Okay," he said, straightening his clothes and standing straight. "Now that we've settled that, let's play ball."

He retrieved the ball and handed it to Ben.

"Your turn this time," Rob said to him, backing away. "Show me what you got! Come on. Toss it to Kane."

Ben rolled the ball around in his hand, examining it but made no effort to toss it.

"Come on, Ben!" Rob encouraged him. "You gotta give it a good, strong, throw. Show Becky what you're made of. Give Kane a chance to catch it!"

At first reluctantly, Ben wound his arm up for a pitch but instead of throwing the ball to Kane, he followed Becky's example and threw it at Rob.

"Whoa!" Rob shouted as he caught the ball. "That's the idea, but wait . . . ."

Reaching into the breast pocket of his shirt, he pulled out his cell phone.

"Yeah," he said, looking closely at the screen of his phone. "Hold on a minute while I put this in the house. The way you guys are throwing that ball, it's liable to get smashed."

Becky laughed.

"Here, Ben," Rob said and lightly tossed the ball to him. "Throw the ball to Kane. See if he'll catch it. Go ahead. I'll be right back."

Rob trotted into the house. He found the three ladies busy preparing a spaghetti dinner.

"How's the game going?" Elizabeth asked, stirring a pan full of meat.

"I left Kane in charge for a minute," he said, tossing his phone on the table. "I'm headed back out there."

Rob moved in next to her and removed a strand of uncooked spaghetti from a box on the sink, sticking it into his mouth, crunching it gingerly.

"Your job is to clean up *after* dinner, not before!" Elizabeth scolded him. "Oh, and since you're here, you can set the table before you go back to play."

Rob nodded and gave her a wink as he reached for the cabinet door above the sink. He was in no hurry to get back to the game of fetch outside.

In the backyard, Ben was still looking at the ball in his hand.

"Come on, Ben," Becky said impatiently. "Throw the ball to Kane. You don't have to wait until Rob gets back. Go ahead."

Ben frowned slightly but didn't move.

"Here, let me show you," Becky said. "First, take two steps backward before you throw it. That's the way real baseball players do it."

Taking him by the shoulders, she started to move Ben backward, but he immediately pulled away from her.

"Okay, but you've got to move back so you can get a good throw," Becky said to him.

Ben continued to hold the ball, eliciting a sigh of impatience from Becky. As she was about to give up on him, he turned around and took two steps toward the fence behind him before stopping and turning back to face Kane. He was at an angle that didn't allow for a straight throw to the dog, and once again he stood without moving.

"Ben, come on," Becky moaned. "Throw it. Throw it, *please*! Kane's waiting."

"That's okay," Kane thought. "I'll wait for him as long as I have to."

A strong gust of wind pushed Ben off balance, as if encouraging him to action. It was an effort to remain on his feet. Once he regained his balance, he took two steps forward and with surprising strength gave the ball a mighty throw. The combined force of his pitch, aided by the powerful blast of a tailwind sent the ball high in the air over Kane's head and the gate behind him into the front yard.

Ben stood staring at the gate, amazed by his own strength.

"Wow!" Becky marveled. "That was *some* throw!"

Becky waited for Ben to retrieve the ball but he made no effort to do so.

"OK," she told him. "You threw it, you gotta go get it. Go on, Ben."

Ben made no move.

"Oh, come on, then," Becky said with a labored sigh as she walked toward the gate. "Come on. I'll go with you. Kane, you can come too."

Pulling the wire that unlatched gate, Becky swung it open wide and gestured for Ben to follow. After some consideration, Ben headed toward it with Kane at his side, but as they passed through the opening, the dog suddenly stopped.

The wind was blowing strongly toward the front of the house in the direction they were heading, but now, intermittently, despite the wind, Kane picked up an alarming scent. At first uncertain, he strained to confirm what his sense of smell was telling him.

"Come on, Kane!" Becky said to him impatiently.

Nervously, Kane trotted ahead to catch up to Ben as Becky followed.

Kane stopped again on the front lawn, holding his nose high in the air to better distinguish the many scents buffeted about by the wind, but he was unable to pinpoint the origin of the smell, and it worried him.

He surveyed the scene before him. Rob's car was parked in the street in front of the lawn. Across the street, a young woman had just parked her car against the curb and was entering the front door of her house. A white sedan was parked several houses away. There was no visible sign of danger, and yet Kane remained uneasy.

"Here it is!" Becky called out to Ben, pointing to a spot next to the curb just behind Rob's car. "Come get it, Ben. Come on."

Picking up the ball, she held it out toward Ben. Slowly, he took it from her.

"Okay," Becky said as she started to walk back toward the gate, "let's throw the ball to Kane."

Unexpectedly, Ben quickly threw the ball, but again it was misdirected, and it sailed high over Kane's head and landed in the street several houses away, bouncing a couple of times before rolling and coming to rest underneath the white sedan.

"Ben!" Becky snapped. "I didn't mean throw it *now*. Not out here. Wait 'til we go in the backyard. Now we've got to go get it."

Kane barked and trotted toward the ball before Becky finished her sentence. He didn't want them going any further from the house. There was something in the area that was not safe, he knew, and if anyone was going to retrieve the ball it should be him, he thought.

"Okay, Kane," Becky called after him. "You go. We'll wait here. Good boy."

Glancing about nervously as he headed toward the white car, Kane noticed that the smell he was trying to identify had grown fainter, but he couldn't be certain if it was because of the wind or because the danger had passed.

Reaching the car, he knelt down and spotted the ball resting against the curb. The vehicle was parked too firmly against the curb for him to retrieve it from that side. He had to crawl beneath it to get the ball, but the car was built somewhat close to the ground, and it took some effort on Kane's part to inch his way close enough to grab the object.

As Becky and Ben watched Kane from down the street, they didn't notice movement in the area behind them, two houses down on the same side of the road where they stood. The driveway in front of that house was hidden behind a barrier of juniper trees, and from that driveway, a black Lincoln Navigator silently rolled into view. When it had cleared the trees, it stopped.

Suddenly there came a loud roar from the SUV's engine, followed by the sound of screeching tires as the vehicle turned sharply into the street and accelerated toward the two children.

Beneath the car, the ball in his mouth, Kane heard the fearful noise, and panic filled his heart as he realized the danger that sound signaled. With extraordinary effort, he dragged himself from beneath the car, as his back scraped beneath its undercarriage.

Clearing himself, he saw the SUV headed in his direction. It swerved sharply to the left, to the curb where the children stood. Kane dropped the ball as the driver's door swung wide. The driver jumped out, grabbed Becky by the arms and flung her across the front seat into the passenger's side. He jumped back in, threw the car into reverse and pulled a U-turn, nearly capsizing in the process.

Kane hardly had time to react, but as the SUV raced away with another screech of tires, Kane sounded the alarm, barking fiercely as he chased after it. He recognized the driver all right. It was the demon, Rodney Hawkins.

Inside the house, Elizabeth dropped the spoon she held in her hand as she and her mother exchanged startled looks. They knew that bark, and it meant danger. Very serious danger.

Without a word between them, both ran to the front door, Rob and Pauline right behind them.

They were just in time to see Kane as he ran by in pursuit of the SUV.

Not sure at first what they were witnessing, it took a moment before they realized anyone was missing.

"Where's Becky?" Elizabeth called out to Ben as she grabbed him by the shoulders and turned him to face her. "Where is she?"

The alarm in Elizabeth's voice combined with the sudden action he had just seen startled the boy. With a low, moaning sound he pointed in the direction Kane was headed.

Pauline screamed her daughter's name as they watched the SUV make a hard right before it disappeared. Kane was right behind it.

Rob rushed to his car, followed by Elizabeth.

"Call 9-1-1!" he yelled out to May over his shoulder. Elizabeth jumped into the front seat before Rob started his car engine and floorboarded the accelerator, headed after the kidnapper.

It wasn't a straight shot to the freeway. There were several turns that needed to be negotiated, and if the kidnapper took the wrong one, he could hit a dead end. Rob could only hope.

"See if you can get the police on the phone," Rob said.

"I don't have my phone," Elizabeth said quickly. "Where's yours?"

"Damn it! I left mine in the kitchen," he said with exasperation.

"Hold tight," Rob warned as his car slid around a corner.

Not far ahead, Kane was losing ground in his pursuit of the SUV, but he and Elizabeth had taken many walks through this neighborhood. He knew that a block ahead of him the road made two right turns, doubling back on itself to run parallel with the street he was on but in the exact opposite direction, one block over. If Kane could cross through the yards of the two houses that sat on the property between him and the next street over, he figured he might make it in time to intercept Becky and her captor. Instantly, he put his plan into action and ran toward a five-foot chain-link gate that enclosed the backyard of the first house in his path. He jumped the gate with relative ease, startling an elderly lady who stood on the other side, watering a bed of roses. She turned the water on Kane, but he paid no attention to her as he raced toward the six-foot brick wall that separated her yard from her neighbor in back. Though he couldn't completely clear the fence, he was able to jump high enough to pull himself up and over.

He came down hard on the other side, hitting a concrete decking, nearly falling into a large swimming pool. Gaining control of himself, he pulled back from the edge of the pool and made his way around the perimeter to the front of the house. A small terrier, laying on a lounge chair on the opposite side of the pool suddenly jumped to his feet, barking ferociously but making no effort to leave the chair. The wooden gate was of equal height to the wall, and once again Kane had to perform a desperate leap he would otherwise not have attempted had it not been for Becky. It took two attempts, but he managed to pull it off.

The grass-covered front yard he landed in was elevated four feet higher than the front sidewalk and the small grass parkway it overlooked and was supported by a brick wall. From the edge of the yard, Kane could see the SUV half a block away as it rounded the corner and raced in his direction. With no time to spare, the dog rushed to the back of the front lawn to prepare for a run at the vehicle as it sped by. His timing would have to be perfect in order to cover the distance between him and the street before leaping up from the edge of the yard, over the sidewalk and parkway to the top of the speeding vehicle. A leap made too early, too late, too low or too short would prove fatal. Kane had no time to consider the odds. He darted across the lawn and with a mighty lunge, propelled himself upward at the precise moment the SUV blew by.

His leap was only high enough to allow him to wrap his front paws around the sidebars of the luggage rack that encircled the roof, leaving his hindquarters dangling down the side of the vehicle. His back feet scratched frantically at the back passenger window as he desperately tried to pull himself upward.

The sound of Kane's toenails scratching the window startled Hawkins. He quickly glanced over his shoulder, an involuntary movement that caused him to jerk the wheel swiftly to the right before regaining control. The abrupt swerve was just fast enough to hurl Kane upward and onto the roof.

Hawkins shouted a profanity as Becky, huddled in the seat beside him, began to scream.

"Shut up! Shut up!" Hawkins yelled, striking her arm with the back of his fist. She screamed louder.

Kane kept low to the roof as the speed of the SUV created a turbulent wind that whipped his fur. Hawkins skidded sharply around every corner, hoping to lose the animal but the luggage rack was just high enough to stop Kane from flying off the side.

The traffic light ahead was red. A steady stream of cross traffic prevented him from barreling through. Instead, he slammed his foot down hard on the brake, skidding to a stop with such force that Kane was sent tumbling headlong to the SUV's hood. He landed in a position facing the windshield, staring directly at the driver, who was startled by the snarling face on the other side of the glass. The sight of the dog cheered Becky, and for a moment, she forgot the pain in her arm.

Kane wasted no time scrambling back to the roof, his feet scraping the windshield as he climbed upward. At the moment Kane regained his position, Hawkins spotted a break in the cross traffic. He jammed the accelerator, simultaneously swinging his vehicle sharply to the left to enter the lane that would lead him to the nearby freeway onramp. Kane slid right, where his front paws slipped beneath the metal bars of the roof rack up to his chest, holding his body and preventing him from being thrown off the side.

It was only a momentary break and one block ahead, in order to access the freeway onramp, Hawkins once again made an abrupt turn, this time to the left, hitting his brakes with such force that the right front tire left the road. The move finally caused Kane to lose his hold, and he was pitched over the sidebars of the roof rack, hitting the pavement with a sickening thud. He rolled into the gutter, stunned and unable to move. The SUV rapidly disappeared up the onramp.

Several cars that had been following behind Hawkins's SUV skidded to a stop, startled by the activity, and a traffic jam began to build. Rob's car was in the midst of the congestion.

"Damn!" he shouted as he honked his horn.

"Wait!" Elizabeth commanded. Squinting her eyes, she could see two people leave their cars to approach an animal which lay in the gutter. She recognized the color of the animal's fur.

"Kane!" she screamed as she jumped from the car and ran down the sidewalk toward him. Rob left his vehicle double-parked and raced to catch up with her.

Elizabeth, almost in tears, was soon kneeling beside Kane's still body.

"Are you all right, boy?" she asked.

At the sound of her voice, his eyes opened with a start. He tried to lift himself, but dizziness kept him off his feet.

"Oh no, Rob," she said. "He's hurt."

Rob knelt beside her.

"He'll be okay, won't you boy?" he asked hopefully, but he was as worried as she was.

It took every bit of his energy for Kane to pull himself back up on his feet.

"There," Rob grinned. "See? He's tough, aren't you, boy?"

Kane wasn't so sure. When he tried to walk, he could only stagger.

"Easy," Elizabeth told him. "Slow and easy."

Kane followed her advice and moved slowly. He staggered just far enough to reach a patch of grass and gratefully laid himself down. The grass was cool and comforting. He wanted to tell them to forget about him and go after Hawkins, but he didn't have the strength to bark, which only added to his guilt. He'd known Hawkins was lying in wait and he'd failed to stop him. He'd never forgive himself if anything happened to Becky.

"We'd better get him to the vet," Rob suggested.

Suddenly, Kane was back on his feet.

"No, Kane!" Elizabeth yelled.

She grabbed for his neck, but he moved too fast for her to get a firm grip and he broke free, heading across the street to the freeway entrance.

As Kane limped across traffic, a sedan swerved to avoid him. Elizabeth rushed into the street with hand held high to halt traffic until the dog could cross.

Pausing at the onramp, Kane took one look at all of the cars, then quickly took the sidewalk that led up and over the freeway. He hadn't traveled more than a few feet when he pulled himself up by the rail to view the freeway below through heavy metal bars. Elizabeth knelt beside him as Rob, having retrieved his car, pulled to the shoulder and ran to join them, prompting several drivers to honk their horns.

The view Kane beheld filled his heart with despair. The evening darkness had begun to fall and stretched before him was one of Southern California's vast freeways that extended endlessly into the horizon, millions of taillights moving relentlessly forever and away. Kane cried out in anguish and in pain, and his legs gave out beneath him as he realized that Becky was gone and it was his fault.

Elizabeth stroked Kane's fur as his cry echoed through the night air.

CHAPTER TWENTY-ONE

Becky vigorously rubbed her arm where Hawkins had slugged her. She did her best to stifle her cries, but the fear and pain kept her sobbing, and no amount of scolding would make her stop as the SUV swerved in and out of traffic at high speed.

Hawkins punched a key on the digital display screen on his dashboard, and his hands-free phone dialed a pre-set number. The response could be heard on his vehicle's speaker.

"Yeah?" a male voice answered.

Hawkins glanced at the girl in the seat beside him before pulling his phone from his pocket, disabling the speaker.

"I got her," he said holding the phone to his ear.

"Hawkins?" said the voice. "What do you mean you got her? Did you . . . ?"

"Not yet," Hawkins said, eyeing Becky. She watched him curiously.

"What do you mean, 'Not yet'?" the other man asked. "Did you take care of her or not?"

"I need someplace to hide her for a while," Hawkins said.

"Hide her? Damn it, you idiot. You weren't supposed to take her prisoner! That wasn't what we planned. What the hell are you thinking?"

"Listen, I got some plans of my own. See, I figure I keep her . . . ." Hawkins paused and lowered his voice. "I figure I'll keep her alive long enough to collect some ransom money first. So I need her around long enough to prove to 'em I got her. Then, after I got the money, *then* . . . I'll double cross 'em, and I'll finish what we set out to do."

A long string of profanities issued from the phone loud enough that even Becky could hear.

"You shithead!" came the voice from the phone. "I don't think you've got the brains God gave a dirty t-shirt! We need that kid gone. *NOW!* She's a risk to us every day she's alive. The family has no money. You finish this business now before they figure out you've got her."

"Ain't gonna do it," Hawkins said flatly. "Not yet. Not 'til I collect. They'll find the money somehow. Meantime, I need someplace to hide out. I ain't takin' a chance holdin' her at my place. So I need your help. What you got? Don't tell me you ain't got no place. Just remember, if I go to prison I'm takin' everybody with me. You, and . . . ."

"Alright. Alright! Settle down," the voice said. "Give me time to think."

Hawkins scoffed. "You got one minute."

There was a very long pause on the phone before the man spoke again.

Elizabeth and Rob returned with Kane to the house and found a cluster of police cars already parked in front. Light streamed through the open front door, and as soon as Rob brought his car to a stop in the driveway, Elizabeth jumped out and ran into the house, leaving him to assist an extremely depressed collie out of the back seat.

Inside, May was seated on the couch, her arm around a near-hysterical Pauline. The two of them did their best to field questions asked by a somber-faced, older, plain-clothes detective who jotted down their answers in a notebook, while three uniformed policemen stood nearby.

Elizabeth rushed to her mother and the two of them embraced.

"Couldn't you catch them?" Pauline asked with a cry.

Elizabeth shook her head slowly and sorrowfully.

"Black Lincoln Navigator headed east on the 91," came Rob's voice from the doorway where he and Kane had just entered. "Sorry I couldn't get his plates."

The officers turned to face him, and he quickly identified himself and related details of his unsuccessful pursuit of the suspect.

"Detective Lauder," the man in charge introduced himself, shaking Rob's hand. Turning to a subordinate, Lauder ordered him to call in the reported description and direction of the fleeing vehicle.

Surveying the room from the doorway where he stood with his head hung low, Kane spotted Ben, frightened and wide-eyed, seated in a chair by himself in the corner of the room.

"Look, Ben," May said to her son as she saw Kane approaching, "Kane is back."

Ben slid to the floor in front of her chair, throwing his arms around Kane. He held him close as the dog placed his muzzle on the boy's shoulder. The warmth of Ben's hug comforted Kane.

"What does he want with my little girl? What's he going to do to her?" Pauline sobbed.

"The vehicle looks like the same one we scared away earlier today up in the San Gabriel mountains," Rob told the detective. "He could have been stalking us, I don't know. But he ran from us up there, even shot at us when we chased him off. I never got close enough to get a description."

Lauder nodded, a frown on his face.

"Bold S.O.B., making a snatch in broad daylight," he mused. "I never thought I'd say something like this but let's hope this *is* a kidnapping, and not . . . ."

He cleared his throat.

"If it's ransom he's after, we'll hear from him soon enough."

"Ransom?" Pauline sobbed. "I don't have any money to pay a ransom."

Lauder nodded as he considered her words. Turning to Rob, he nodded his head toward the kitchen and the two men headed in that direction.

As they left the room, May did her best to console Pauline and Elizabeth slid down on the floor next to Ben. He wouldn't allow her to touch him, but she offered him words of consolation. Kane took the opportunity to follow Rob and the police lieutenant into the kitchen. They didn't notice as he stood near them, listening.

"What's your thought, Officer?" Lauder asked Rob.

"We need to contact Lieutenant Mosher in Homicide," Rob replied.

A short while later, it was decided that Pauline should return to her apartment in case the kidnapper attempted to contact her. Lauder called for a technical crew to install monitoring equipment in the hope that if a call came through, it could be traced. He placed a second call to Mosher, asking him to meet him at the apartment. There was no doubt that Becky was targeted because she was a witness to her father's murder and that connection led them to conclude that the kidnapper was likely to be Rodney Hawkins. An Amber Alert was promptly issued, posting a description of Hawkins and his vehicle.

Rob offered to drive Pauline home and to stay to provide support as they waited for the next development. Elizabeth remained behind to comfort her mother, but as Rob escorted Pauline to the door, Ben rushed up to them.

"Take Kane," Ben said to Pauline. "You need him right now."

May covered her mouth with her hand. She had nearly forgotten about her son during the chaos that had been taking place, and this sudden gesture of generosity touched her deeply and made her proud. Though she couldn't say how it was, some inner voice told her that Ben was going to be okay and that his cancer would not win. It was the closest she had ever come to a religious experience.

"Oh, Ben," Elizabeth sighed as she knelt next to her brother. "That is so wonderfully sweet of you, but . . . ."

"No," he said firmly. "Becky's mother is very sad now. Kane makes people feel better. She needs him until Becky comes back home."

Kane knew his boy was right. He stepped away from his family and stood next to Pauline.

"I'll look after him," Rob assured Elizabeth. "And when . . . when we get Becky back, I'll return him to you."

Ben retrieved the plastic Godzilla from an end table next to the couch and began moving the toy's arms and legs into various positions.

Rob managed to give Elizabeth a wink before making his exit with Pauline and Kane.

CHAPTER TWENTY-TWO

At Pauline's apartment, a phone recording device and tracing equipment had been installed on the kitchen table, and a uniformed officer was busy making final adjustments. Two others sat nearby, sipping coffee they had picked up on their way from the McLaughlin's temporary residence.

Pauline paced nervously and Lauder reviewed his notes and fielded phone calls while Rob sat nearby, scratching Kane's ear.

Kane watched Pauline.

An officer leaned in the door and called out to Lauder.

"Sir. A Lieutenant Mosher from Homicide to see you," he announced.

Lauder motioned for Rob to join him and they stepped outside to find Mosher standing on the front lawn, surveying the neighborhood. Introductions were made and Kane, unnoticed, stood in the doorway, within listening distance.

"We sent a car around to Hawkins' place," Mosher told them. "'Course he wasn't there. Didn't expect him to be. Our boys asked around the neighborhood, but it's not too friendly a place as you can pretty well imagine. For the little girl's sake, I just hope to hell he's not the one that nabbed her, but it's a pretty safe bet he's our guy. Oh, and there's one other thing. Take a look at this."

Mosher led them to his car, parked at the curb. Rob's face lit up when he saw his old pal Danny Ralston leaning against the vehicle, puffing on a cigarette, as usual.

"I hope this wasn't what you wanted to show us," Rob said with a smile as he pointed to Danny.

"Who's your partner?" Danny asked, nodding toward Kane.

"Show 'em what you found," Mosher said as he waved away a cloud of Danny's freshly exhaled smoke.

Danny tossed his unfinished cigarette to the curb and reached through the window of the car, withdrawing a laptop computer, which he set up on the hood and prepared for display.

"I got to thinking," Danny said hoarsely, "which, despite what you might think, is what I get paid to do from time to time, just as long as I don't overdo it."

"Cut the crap, Ralston," Mosher ordered.

"OK, somebody beat us to the video of the visitor at the liquor store Becky saw on the night Burton was murdered," Danny continued, unphased. "So who got ahold of that video? Well, I paid another visit to the liquor store guy who, by the way, is awful sick of seein' us comin' around. Says it's bad for business. Anyway, I had him check for me and, sure enough, he found what I was lookin' for. See, our unknown visitor snatched the video taken that night but what he didn't get was the video that recorded him picking up the video!"

Danny made an elaborate gesture before hitting the "enter" key on the computer and then stood aside proudly to display the video. When a blank screen failed to produce an image, Mosher sighed impatiently and Danny nervously fiddled with the flash drive on the device until a video image finally appeared.

The picture on the screen was at first difficult to distinguish, but as the viewers' eyes adjusted, they could finally make out the back of a man in a light-colored suit as he approached the counter. He pulled something from his coat pocket and showed it to the clerk.

"A liquor store with only one camera. Go figure. But don't worry," Danny assured them, "We got his face. I made an edit so you wouldn't have to watch the whole thing. Watch this!"

As he spoke, the clerk handed a small object, assumed to be a flash drive, to the man in front of him. The man collected it, and the camera caught his face on his way out.

Danny, once more with elaborate ceremony, clicked the "pause" key.

Kane turned and re-entered the house.

"I'll be damned!" Rob said. "I saw that guy at headquarters, and the other night. He was here."

"Richard Teller," Danny said proudly, as he lit another cigarette. "Right-hand man to Mayor Robbins himself."

Rob and Lauder stood for a moment trying to absorb the information they had just been given.

"I'll ask the same question I asked the other night when he was here," Rob said finally. "What is the mayor's interest in Zach's murder?"

"Teller could have been the guy the little girl saw that night," Mosher remarked.

"If only we knew what Zach knew," Rob said pointedly.

Mosher nodded.

"Must be some pretty explosive stuff," he said. "If I was smart, I'd keep out of this mess but, dammit, maybe it's time I stuck my neck out for once."

"You could be asking for trouble," Lauder said.

"Tell me something I don't know," Mosher replied, laughing.

"See," Danny said to Rob. "I told you he wasn't *all* bad."

"Shut up, Ralston," Mosher said irritably. "And put out that damn cigarette!"

"Why don't you show Officer Martinez what you got for him?" Danny asked flashing a big grin as he threw away his cigarette and retrieved another from his pocket.

"Oh, yeah," Mosher said, opening the door to his car. Reaching into the glovebox, he withdrew Rob's weapon and badge and handed them to him.

"The captain said I should give this back to you," Mosher said. "Your administrative leave is over. We both figure we need you workin' with us on this. So you're reporting to me for the time being."

"You're starting to look a lot better to me," Rob said, taking his gun and shield.

Mosher frowned back at him.

" . . . Sir," Rob added with respect.

"Excuse me, Rob?" Pauline called from the doorway. "Would you come take a look at this please?"

"Sure," he replied. Nodding to Mosher, he turned to join her. Lauder remained with Mosher and Danny.

As Pauline led him toward Becky's bedroom, Rob heard a commotion originating from that direction.

He was startled to find Kane, using his front paw, to pull books off the bookshelf onto the floor. He watched the dog scratch at the pages before pulling another book from the shelf, leaving a tousled and mangled mess in a pile on the carpet.

"Kane!" Rob started, "What the hell are you . . . ?"

He stopped mid-sentence. The dog was looking for something. After pawing through the pages, unable to find what he was seeking, he would continue his search, pulling another book from the shelf before trying another.

It didn't take long for him to find "The Heart of a Dog" by Albert Payson Terhune. The large, aging volume fell to the floor, and the edge of the envelope that Becky had hidden lay partially exposed behind the cover of the book. With his mouth, Kane pulled it free and turned to Rob.

Kane knew he was breaking his promise to Becky, but under the new circumstances, he knew it must be an important link to the creature who had kidnapped her, and he felt compelled to break his oath.

Rob removed the envelope from Kane's mouth and examined the writing on the front.

"That's Zach's handwriting!" Pauline exclaimed.

"What's going on?" Mosher asked, joining them. Danny was close behind.

Rob turned to him and handed him the envelope on which the name, "CAPTAIN TAKIMOTO" was written, and underneath it, the word, "CONFIDENTIAL."

Reaching into his pocket, Mosher removed a pocket knife and used one of its blades to unseal the envelope.

CHAPTER TWENTY-THREE

Dear Sir

I am providing this letter for your review during our meeting in which I intend to present evidence of my ongoing investigation into the operations of

Los Angeles gangs involved in the high level dealing of illicit drugs. As the facts and details will prove, this operation includes virtually all of the gangs in our city, in league with select members of law enforcement and city officials. This unholy alliance can be traced all the way to the head of our city government. To be specific, Mayor Edward Robbins himself.

Before you write me off as a lunatic or worse, I ask that you first examine the evidence. The information will detail an agreement that has been made between Administrative Assistant Richard Teller on behalf of Mayor Robbins with Rodney Hawkins and other gang leaders, which gives each of them permission to operate their illegal operations within specific, designated districts. The agreement stipulates that if any gang is caught performing operations in an area allocated by the mayor for a rival gang, the offending member(s) will be the target of lethal force by law enforcement.

This arrangement serves a dual purpose. By allowing law enforcement to provide punishment, the mayor is seen by the public as being tough on crime while *at the same time, the absence of gang-on-gang retaliation shows the public that the mayor has managed to clean up the streets of L.A. Meanwhile, the gangs move their drugs without fear of arrest.*

More importantly, aside from the public relations benefit the mayor's office will reap, in exchange for this protection, the gangs provide the mayor with a sizeable percentage of all sales of illegal narcotics.

This activity has been going on for a few years and, up to this point, has been highly successful. Inevitably, however, the details of this operation were bound to be discovered, and since I have uncovered these facts, I fear for my life. Consequently, the evidence I will be providing you has been temporarily turned over to an individual whose confidentiality I trust implicitly. I will retrieve it from him for your review prior to our meeting. However, in the event that I am prevented, for whatever reason, from meeting with you, I urge you to personally contact the individual whose name and information appears at the bottom of this letter. Do not be fooled or alarmed by your first impression of this man. I have worked with him for a considerable amount of time, and despite his criminal history, he has proven himself to me to be reliable and honest and is committed to seeing justice done.

My decision to turn this information over to you is based on my years of experience under your command

and my confidence in your honesty, integrity, and bravery and I believe leadership at the Federal level will be more likely to consider these accusations if someone of your rank presents them.

I don't have the names of every law enforcement official who may be involved in this operation, but I fear some may even operate within your own department, so I urge the utmost caution when choosing with which individuals you will share these details.

Until our meeting, I remain

Respectfully yours,

Zach Burton

The contact information shown at the bottom of the letter referred to the name, James Morris.

CHAPTER TWENTY-FOUR

Sitting on the bed in Becky's room, Detective Mosher looked around him. Rob, Pauline, Detective Lauder and Danny all stood in silence as they grappled with the enormity of the accusations detailed in the letter he had just read to them. As his hand began to shake slightly, he placed it on the bed and rubbed his cheek.

"Okay," he said finally, "What you just heard doesn't leave this room. For your own safety. Not until we've got that evidence in our hands and we know for sure this is all real. Everybody got me?"

"If the gangs don't get us, the mayor's guys and the bad cops will," Danny mused.

"We're gonna have to grill this guy, Teller," Lauder said. "He must have some clue where the girl's been taken."

"Well, we've been trying to reach him with no luck," Mosher replied. "We've staked out his house and his office so as soon as he shows up, we'll question him but we have to tread lightly. If we tip our hand too soon everyone from the mayor on down will probably lawyer up or . . . ."

Mosher paused. The expression on Pauline's face indicated she was scared. Rob placed a reassuring arm around her shoulders.

"You're not the only one who's got the jitters," he told her.

"OK," Mosher said, picking up the letter. "Let's see if this guy Morris can be of any help."

As he removed his phone from his pocket and started to dial, he asked Rob where he found the letter.

"I didn't," Rob replied and pointed to Kane, who was sitting in the doorway watching. "He did."

Mosher's jaw dropped.

"How in hell," he wondered aloud, "did that dog know we needed this letter?"

He shook his head and continued dialing. After four rings, someone answered.

"Hello," Mosher replied. "I need you to listen carefully to what I have to say. I'm Police Detective Mosher, and this involves Zach Burton and the evidence he left with you. I know you have no reason to trust me, but that information may be key to helping us locate his kidnapped daughter, so I need to talk to you as soon as possible."

There was no response.

"I beg you, sir," Mosher continued. "you're going to have to trust somebody eventually. Please."

"Meet me at the Griffith Park Zoo in one hour," Morris said after a lengthy pause. "You alone?"

"There'll be two other cops with me," Mosher told him. "Nobody else. I promise."

Mosher didn't wait for a reply.

"Martinez, Ralston, come on," Mosher said, shoving the letter into the breast pocket of his coat as he headed for the door. Kane followed after him.

Rob gave Pauline's arm a tight squeeze.

"Keep your chin up," he said to her. "We'll get her back. She'll be OK. I'm sure of it."

As he followed Mosher from the room, he wished he felt as confident as he sounded.

In the front room, he was met by Elizabeth.

"Mom and Ben are doing OK," she told him. "I thought I'd come over here to support Pauline. What's happening?"

"I'm glad you're here," he replied. "Pauline can fill you in. I'll be back in a bit."

"Wait," she said, stopping him. "Are you OK?"

He forced a smile but didn't answer as he turned to go. Elizabeth sensed he was feeling guilty about the fact that Becky was abducted under his watch. She was reminded that someone else was feeling guilty.

"Where's Kane?" she asked.

Pauline pointed to the front door.

Mosher ordered Danny to drive but stopped when he noticed Rob holding the back door for Kane to enter.

"Wait a minute," Mosher yelled out. "What the hell do you think you're doing?"

"You're gonna have to trust me on this one," Rob replied. "This dog has been instrumental in this case from the very beginning. I gotta figure if he thinks it's important to go with us, I'm trusting his judgment."

Mosher started to protest, but Danny interrupted.

"Why not?" he asked. "We're going to the zoo, right?"

Mosher slid into the car, slammed the door and muttered a profanity.

Detective Mosher and his group found the parking lot outside the Griffith Park Zoo empty but well illuminated. It was about 9:00 PM. The wind was not blowing as heavily in that part of town, but it remained constant. Cruising the lot, they eventually spotted an early model blue Honda Civic, badly in need of a body shop makeover, parked near a wide walkway which led to the main entrance to the zoo. Pulling up next to the vehicle, they found it empty.

Motioning for Rob and Danny to follow, Mosher got out of the car to look for the man they had come to meet, but when Kane prepared to join them, Mosher waved him back.

"Leave the dog," he ordered.

Hesitant at first, Rob complied, but not before rolling down the window. Placing his fingers to his lips, he winked at Kane and joined the others.

Kane watched nervously as the group departed. Why, he thought, did they bring him only to leave him behind? Did they think the only thing he wanted was a ride? Humans weren't as smart as they thought they were.

As the men negotiated the walkway, they failed to notice the heavy-set man seated on a bench amid a growth of shrubbery nearby.

"Hey!" the man called out quietly.

The man was sitting casually, his hands inside a thin coat. They approached him cautiously.

"Your name James Morris?" Mosher addressed him.

Morris nodded.

"We need to cut through the crap if you don't mind," Mosher began. "We've got a kidnapped little girl we need to get back to her mother and if you're the friend Zach Burton claims you've been, you're gonna want to give us any information you've got. Zach intended to turn it over to Captain Takimoto, and we'll make sure that happens."

178

"I don't know," Morris replied, eyeing them suspiciously. "How do I know I can trust you with it?"

"You don't," Mosher said. "But you'll have to. What can we do to prove we're on your side?"

Morris studied his face for a moment before shaking his head.

"I don't know, man," he said. "I'm a pretty good judge of character, and I'm just not too sure about you."

After a long pause, Morris stood.

"I gotta think about this," he said, turning to go.

"We don't have time!" Mosher said, drawing his gun. "I don't want to have to use this, but I can't let you walk away!"

Morris stopped.

"That's how we're gonna play it, huh?" he asked defiantly. "That ain't gonna do you no good. I don't have what you're lookin' for on me right now anyway, so you're gonna have to wait until I decide to give it to you. *If* I decide to give it to you."

Behind the fence surrounding the zoo and some distance away, the sound of a roaring lion could be heard as Morris sneered at the detective and again turned to leave. He had taken several steps before Mosher raised his firearm.

"Hold it!" he yelled, but he was ignored.

"Mosher!" Rob called out as he stepped forward, fully prepared to stop him.

"Stay back, Martinez!" Mosher yelled. "Morris! I'm giving you until the count of three before I pull this trigger. You hear me?"

Morris shook his head and continued on.

"One! Two . . . ."

Suddenly Morris stopped. Kane was running toward him. His fur shimmered in the wind as he approached.

"Wait. I know that dog. Kane!" Morris called out. "Is that you, boy?"

Mosher looked at Rob who smiled and shrugged.

Morris knelt down and greeted his friend with a warm hug.

"How you been, boy?" he asked. "Damn it's good to see you again!"

Roughing his fur, Morris stayed with Kane for a while before finally rising and turning to the men behind him.

"Is Kane with you guys?" he asked.

Mosher lowered his weapon.

"Uh . . . yeah," he replied.

"Where's the lady that owns him?" Morris asked.

"Right now she's with Zach's wife waiting for the kidnapper to call," Rob answered.

Looking down at Kane, Morris said, "I met her and Kane while I was in jail. Well, OK then. I guess if Kane can trust you, so can I. But it's probably gonna get me in a lot of trouble."

"With who?" Mosher asked.

"With Rodney Hawkins, to begin with," Morris responded.

"That's who we're looking for," Rob said anxiously. "He's the kidnapper."

"Can't help you there," Morris said shaking his head. "I know he ain't hangin' out in any of his usual spots. I can do my best to ask around but I ain't been too popular lately. It ain't likely I'm gonna find out too much."

180

"What about the goods Zach left with you?" Mosher asked.

Morris nodded toward the bench on which he had been sitting. He reached underneath and retrieved a computer flash drive which had been taped there.

"Everything you want is right there," he said, handing it to Rob. "Lotta people gonna be pretty upset when that gets out. Hope you're ready for what comes next."

"Why did he trust you with this?" Rob said, clutching the flash drive tightly in his fist.

"Zach and me go way back," Morris said, his eyes slightly misty. "He did more for me than anybody I ever knew. I helped him out when I could. I just wish I coulda helped him when he needed it most."

Kneeling again, he placed his arm around Kane's neck.

"Yeah," he said quietly in Kane's ear. "Zach gave me a puppy a few years back. That dog grew up to be my best friend before the cops shot her. Now she's gone, and Zach's gone. I ain't got nobody now."

CHAPTER TWENTY-FIVE

Finally, the call that Pauline and Detective Lauder been expecting came through at about 10:30 PM. Pauline jumped, startled by the ring of the phone and then rushed to the device which sat on an end table beside the sofa where she had been sitting with Elizabeth.

Lauder motioned for her to wait before picking up. He signaled the officer in the kitchen who nodded and activated the phone equipment.

"Go ahead," he told Pauline.

Anxiously, she answered the call, but she was so nervous she could barely manage to say, "Hello."

"Your little girl gave me your number," she heard Hawkins say. "I know we're not alone on this call, Missus Burton, but it don't matter anyway 'cause this phone is one of those burners. Can't be traced. So tell your friends there that they're wastin' their time."

"What do you want?" Pauline asked, stifling a sob. "Is my baby OK?"

"Oh, she's fine," he replied, "for now, anyway. But you're gonna have to get busy real quick on Facebook and Twitter and such and maybe that 'Go Fund Me' website to raise some money so she can come back to you. When folks start hearin' about your kid and how she's in danger and all, I figure you're gonna be able to get your hands on a whole lot of cash."

"Where is she? Put her on the phone!" she demanded, suddenly overwhelmed with rage.

Lauder was taken aback.

There was a pause at the other end of the line as she heard Hawkins' muffled voice talking to someone nearby. Finally, she heard a small, frightened voice call out to her.

"Mommy?" Becky said.

"Baby!" Pauline shouted with desperation. "Are you OK, honey? Has anybody hurt you?"

"Mommy, I'm afraid," Becky said loudly. "He told me I have to stay inside 'cause there's a big bear outside someplace. A sign said so."

Before Pauline could respond, the phone was yanked away.

"That'll do for now," Hawkins said. "All you need to know is five hundred thousand. That's the magic number. Once word of this gets out, I figure you won't have no problem gettin' that much together. I'm givin' you, oh, let's say, twenty-four hours. Then I'll call you back, and let you know how this is gonna work. So you get busy now, and I'll be in touch. Have a good evenin'."

The connection was broken.

The officer at the phone equipment shook his head at Lauder who threw his earphones down angrily.

"Missus Burton," he started to say.

"I've got to get busy," Pauline said, jumping up and walking toward her bedroom door. "You heard what he said. I've got to get on the computer and raise that money. Elizabeth, can you phone the TV stations? Maybe they'll help us get the word out."

"Hold on," Lauder said, but Pauline ignored him as she headed for the computer in her bedroom. Simultaneously, Rob and Kane returned from their meeting with Morris.

"Where's Mosher?" Lauder asked. "Did you get what you needed?"

"Looks like it," Rob replied. "He and Ralston are headed back to the station to put it all together. What's going on?"

Lauder handed Rob his earphones as he nodded for the tech officer to play back the phone call. Danny listened intently as Kane, sitting next to him, cocked his head, trying to hear. When the recording ended, Rob handed the earphones back to Lauder.

" I wonder what the bear thing is all about?" Rob wondered.

"She said she saw a sign, warning about bears," Lauder recalled.

Rob thought in silence a moment.

"No. Not '*bears*,'" he said finally. "She said, a '*big bear*.'"

Anxiously, he pulled his phone and selected a pre-programmed number.

"What is it, Rob?" Elizabeth asked.

"Danny!" Rob said into the phone. "I think we've got something. How quick do you think you can locate all the property Teller owns? Yeah, I need it quick."

While Danny researched, Elizabeth began placing phone calls to local television news stations.

"You know, we don't recommend paying extortion demands," Lauder told her. Before she could cast him an angry glance, he added, "I have to tell you that. It's my job."

He waited for her to leave the room before saying, "The minute he gets his hands on that money, that kid is as good as dead."

Kane was nervously pacing. It didn't seem like anyone was doing enough. Had they forgotten Becky? Who the devil was in charge?

Slightly less than an hour later, Danny called back.

"I got three locations. Which one do you want first?" he asked.

"Any chance he owns a place in Big Bear?" Rob replied.

"Damn, you're good!" Danny declared as he rattled off an address.

Hastily jotting down the information Danny read to him, Rob promised to be in touch and hung up.

"You can follow me and my crew," Lauder said, copying the address into his notepad. "I don't like doing this at night. If this is a country cabin, he'll see our lights approaching a mile away. We might have to stay back a bit until daybreak. We can figure it out when we get there."

Pauline rushed into the room, clutching her purse.

"You'd be better off . . . ." Lauder started to say.

"Don't tell me I'd be better off staying here," she interrupted. "You know damn well I'm not going to do that!"

"Yeah, I know," he replied, "but it's another one of those things I'm supposed to say in these situations. You'll have to ride with Officer Martinez."

"And me," Elizabeth added.

"OK," Lauder said tentatively, then added sarcastically, "Anybody else going?"

"Yes, Kane is going," Rob replied as he headed out the door.

Lauder rolled his eyes as he pulled his phone from his pocket and placed a call to headquarters.

Kane beat the others to the car door, and as he waited for them to catch up, he saw Morris' dilapidated blue Civic, parked at the curb about half a block away. It followed them. Kane was sure it would. He watched it through the rear window and nudged Elizabeth's arm with his muzzle, but she was lost in worry and didn't notice. Kane was determined to get her attention, so he barked.

"What?" she asked.

Kane looked out the window, his ears up, looked back at her, and again at the window.

"What's wrong?" Rob asked.

"I don't know, she said, stroking Kane's back. "Just anxious I guess."

"Join the club," Rob said glibly.

Kane barked again, looking back and forth from Elizabeth to the window.

"Now, that's enough!" she said firmly.

Kane gave in and lay in her lap, sulking.

Humans!

Rob stuck closely behind Detective Lauder's vehicle, whose flashing red lights allowed for extra speed on the route that would normally take over two hours. Before long they were joined by an escort of four marked police cars, their sirens blaring while winds buffeted them about the freeway. Soon afterward, Rob's phone rang, and he answered on his car speaker.

"I got some bad news for you folks," they heard Lauder's voice say.

Rob looked at Pauline, who was steeling herself for the information.

"There's a fire. A bad one. The whole area's been evacuated," Lauder continued. "I'm not sure if we'll be able to get in."

CHAPTER TWENTY-SIX

The night sky was illuminated by the flames of the deadly forest fire that burned in the distance, as Rob and his escort traveled the road that would eventually lead them to the cabin where they believed Becky was being held. Rounding a curve, they were met with a police roadblock.

A base camp of operations had been set up in an adjoining field where tents had been erected, holding their own against the fierce wind amid motorhomes, generators, food trucks, buses, fire trucks and other firefighting equipment. Temporary lighting illuminated the area where many firefighters rushed about preparing to do battle with the elements while others rested between shifts.

Detective Lauder talked with an officer at the roadblock for a few minutes before turning back to the other members of his group, motioning for them to follow his car into the base camp.

At the camp, they parked where they could between the cars and trucks. Rob nodded toward a group of firefighters blackened by smoke and consumed with exhaustion as they lay on the ground.

"Those guys must have the hardest job in the world," he mused.

Parking his car, Lauder walked toward what appeared to be the command vehicle.

"Why don't you wait here and I'll see what's going on. They may be more willing to cooperate with cops than with civilians," Rob said.

Elizabeth nodded and cast a consoling smile in Pauline's direction as Kane, impatient with the delay, nervously alternated between standing and sitting on the seat beside her. At every stop, he had hoped to see Becky. He'd never been more perplexed in his life.

A group of officers was gathered around a man who appeared to be the captain. He was struggling with a large map, pressing it against a small table as the fierce wind attempted to carry it away. A sudden gust nearly blew it out of their grasp, and every hand quickly came to the rescue.

The captain was in no mood to deal with strangers. When Lauder tried to engage him, the captain dismissed him with a disdainful wave of his hand.

"The cabin shouldn't be too much further from here," Rob said to Lauder, "but from the look of those flames and what I've been hearing on the radio, we'd better not waste any time. Maybe we could . . . . "

"Can I help you gentlemen?" interrupted a female fire captain who stood nearby.

Lauder introduced himself and explained the reason they needed to get up the road. The captain listened patiently.

"I'm Captain Phyllis Tully," she said, shaking their hands. "The commander pretty much has his hands full right now as you can see, but I'll do my best to help. Problem is, there's not much we can do until daylight. We can try to get a unit in there to lead you through, maybe get an air unit to drop some water on the area. Come here and show me where that cabin is,"

They followed the captain into a nearby tent where rolls of maps were scattered about a large table. Tully rummaged through them until she found one that covered the area nearby. Unrolling it on the table, she marked a spot on the map with a pen indicating their present location. Lauder ran his finger along the route, designating the path they needed to take, stopping at the point where the cabin was located.

"There," he said with finality. "That's the place."

Tully frowned as she marked it.

"Hmm," she said ominously. "That's not going to be easy, I'm afraid. The dirt road that leads up there is pretty narrow, which makes it difficult to get heavy equipment in and out. Once we do, if I understand what you're telling me, we won't know what kind of resistance we're going to run into with the suspect. Getting our people and equipment back out of there won't be any too easy either."

She took another look at the map.

"Tell you what," she resumed. "Let me work this out, contact air support and see if we can get a water drop soon as it's light enough. I can give you one bit of good news. The winds are starting to calm a bit so if they don't kick up between now and morning and if they continue in the direction they're headed right now, that might buy us some time, so keep your fingers crossed. Why don't you folks hang out over by the food truck. Get a cup of coffee and some food, and I'll keep you posted."

Rob and Lauder thanked her and headed back to their cars, burdened with the task of informing their companions of the delay.

As she watched them go, Captain Tully wished she could have told them what she really believed. The truth was, it would take a miracle to get to the cabin before the fire did.

The morning light was just dawning as Rodney Hawkins was pacing about Richard Teller's two-room cabin which sat alone amid a high forest at the end of a long dirt road in the hills above Big Bear Lake. It boasted a loft in the main room and was adorned with furniture and embellishments, which, despite their faux, rustic cabin theme, had likely been purchased at a premium.

Becky, fearful and trembling, cowered in the corner of a couch as Hawkins, with a phone against his ear, kicked over an expensive end table and angrily tossed aside a quality chair across the room

"You need to stop whinin' and help me figure out what I'm gonna do next," Hawkins screamed. "Don't be tellin' me how you're in a dangerous situation 'cause it ain't nothin' like the situation you're gonna be in if I get caught or if somethin' happens to me. Listen, if I get killed, my people are gonna find you, and you're gonna wish you was dead too, and if the cops catch me, I'm gonna be puttin' the finger on you, so you'd best be thinkin' fast. I'm up here now, and there's a fire breathin' down my neck. They got Amber Alerts all over the place, and my picture's plastered all over the damn television."

"Okay," Teller was telling him, "I hear what you're saying, and we're going to figure something out. First of all, is the kid still alive?"

"Yeah," Hawkins replied. "She's alive for now."

"Okay," Teller said evenly, "is the road still open for you to get out of there?"

"I don't know," he said, throwing aside a set of curtains and opening a window. "There's fire everywhere out there. It's almost got me surrounded. They probably got the road closed, I don't know."

"Then get out of there now but leave the girl. If the fire is as bad as it looks on TV, she won't make it out alive. There's no proof you're involved, and with my connections, they won't dare . . . ."

"What the hell do I care what happens to you?" Hawkins screamed, louder this time. "Get me outta here. You got the connections!"

"Exactly what do you expect me to do?" Teller asked. "You got yourself into this."

Hawkins was ready to throw his phone at the wall, but his better sense took over. He took a deep breath instead.

"This ain't the time to be pointin' fingers," he said. "I'm gettin' outta here. Meet me at the bottom of the hill."

"I'll be there," Teller assured him.

Hawkins hung up the phone and stood frozen, trying his best not to think of the ordeal ahead of him. For a moment he studied Becky, who was shaking with fear. With a swift jerk, he pulled the phone from the wall. He wasn't taking any chances.

"Are we leaving now?" Becky dared to ask.

He sneered at her and turned to go, but then stopped.

"A towel!" he said. Rushing to the bathroom, he yanked a towel off the rack, dropped it in the sink and turned on the tap. When it was thoroughly saturated, he returned to the living room, with the towel dripping wet.

"What's that for?" Becky dared to ask.

"This? This is my ticket outta here," he proudly announced. "It's my disguise. Nobody'll think nothin' about a guy tryin' to protect himself. They won't recognize me with this across my face."

Becky started toward the bathroom. Hawkins grabbed her arm.

"Where do you think you're goin'?" he asked.

"To get a towel," she said simply.

Hawkins threw her back on the couch.

"You ain't goin' nowhere," he said to her. "Here's what's gonna happen. I'm goin' to get help, you hear? You stay right here in the house where you're safe. Remember what I said about the big bear out there in the woods? Well, now that the fire burned up his house, he's really pissed, and he's gonna be lookin' for some little girl to eat. Soon as he spots you, he's gonna gobble you up for dinner, so you just stay put 'til I get back. You got that? *Stay here!*"

"When will you be back?" she asked, crying.

"You don't worry about that," he answered. "Your momma wants you to stay here, so you do what she says and just sit tight."

Becky hugged a sofa pillow close to her chest as she nodded.

After a quick glance around the room, Hawkins reached in his pocket for his car keys before walking out the door. The finality with which he slammed the door behind him and the sound it made caused Becky to blink. Now it was completely quiet, and the silence in the cabin accentuated the loneliness and fear that engulfed her. A short while later she heard his car engine start, and she rushed to the door to follow.

From the screened-in front porch, she caught a glimpse of Hawkins' SUV as it sped down the dirt road and was soon swallowed up by the forest. She could see the flames of the approaching fire behind the barrier of trees that encircled the cabin. Her imagination began to take hold as she peered into the darkness of the surrounding woods, and she ran back inside, closing the door behind her.

Jumping back on the sofa, she grabbed a lap blanket that lay nearby. As she gathered it around her, there was a sudden pop, and the lights went out. Smoke filled the sky, blotting out what little morning light existed, leaving her in near darkness. The only light came from the glow of the fire outside as its image danced across the walls

Becky never felt more alone in her life, or more certain that she would never see her mother again.

CHAPTER TWENTY-SEVEN

At the firefighters' base camp, Kane had remained close to Elizabeth and Pauline throughout the night. He wanted to tell them everything was going to be OK, and help ease their worry, though he had no way of knowing what lay ahead. At the first hint of morning light, Rob sought out Captain Tully. It was just one of several times he had pestered her for an update. Kane and Lauder joined him. They found the captain deep in conversation with several men near the command vehicle.

"Look, I apologize for bugging you again," Rob interrupted,"but you have to understand we are just plain out of time. We've got to do something right now."

Turning from the group with whom she had been speaking, she looked at Rob and then glanced at the ladies sitting nearby. The expression on her face told Rob that there was no good news. Tully nodded toward the tent, indicating for them to follow her. Once inside, she took a deep breath before speaking.

"I'm not going to sugar coat this," she began. "As I feared, the winds have picked up, and the cabin is right in their path. Even if we were to try to send a team in there, even if that kidnapper doesn't put up a resistance, we can't possibly beat the fire. It's going to get there before we can."

Rob started to speak, but Captain Tully held up a hand to indicate she wasn't finished.

"Now, we've got a helicopter en route to try and dump water on the cabin," she continued, "but they're going in there against orders because the wind is just making it too dangerous to fly. They're very brave men on board, and they know the risk, but they're going to try anyway. They're pretty close to the target and we should be getting an update any minute."

"Maybe he's not at the cabin," Rob said hopefully. "I mean, we don't really know for sure. Maybe he saw the fire start up yesterday and he already got out."

"That's what I was hoping," Tully said. "As soon as it got bright enough to take a picture, we got this satellite image before the helicopter took off."

She opened a laptop computer sitting amid the maps on the table and turned it so they could see the image displayed. Though a bit fuzzy, the picture was clear enough for them to make out one important feature.

"That's his SUV," Rob said with disappointment. "But Hawkins can't be stupid enough to stay there. He's got to be on his way out by now."

"Hopefully," Tully said, "We've got teams stationed all up and down the highway between here and the cutoff to the cabin. That road is the only way out of there, but so far he hasn't been seen. If he's not already on his way, he's probably not going to make it out."

There was a crackling sound on the walkie-talkie the captain wore on her belt. She pulled the device from its holster.

"Go ahead," she commanded.

"I've got the chopper pilot on the line, Captain," a voice replied. "I'm patching him through so you can monitor as requested."

Tully set the walkie-talkie on the table and turned up the volume as Rob and Lauder gathered near. The conversation at first consisted of exchanges between the pilot and an air traffic controller, discussing wind speed and direction. The conditions were formidable, and the base commander repeatedly ordered them to return, but each time the pilot complained that the transmission was breaking up.

For the drop to be effective, it was necessary for the aircraft to get as close to the target as possible. However, the cloud of smoke that encompassed the area was blowing over the forest at a height that made visibility impossible and the lower the helicopter dipped, the more it was pummeled by the wind. With his attention directed toward the cabin, the pilot failed to notice that he had drifted too close to a nearby tree.

"Look out!" a crew member yelled.

In a split second, the pilot banked, narrowly avoiding a fatal error.

With time running out, and the danger increasing with every second, the crew decided to make their best estimate of the target area. They had no choice but to dump the water and hope for the best. Discharging the contents of the water bladder the helicopter was towing, the pilot ascended again and hovered for a moment to analyze the accuracy of the drop.

The mission, as he relayed to the commander in a voice choked with disappointment, was unsuccessful. As the smoke cleared temporarily over the area, the crew watched helplessly as the water missed its mark and, blown by the wind, it landed ineffectively amid a tower of flames to the left of the cabin. With no time left to attempt another run, there was nothing left for them to do but return to the base. The transmission ended, and the rest was silence.

Saying nothing, Tully quietly returned the walkie-talkie to its holster.

"Well, I'm going up there," Rob blurted out, turning to leave the tent. "I'll take my chances."

Tully grabbed his arm.

"Don't be a fool," the captain told him. "You won't get past the roadblock."

"It's my fault she's up there in the first place!" Rob shouted. "If I hadn't been goofing off with my friends, he wouldn't have . . . *she* wouldn't have . . . ."

Rob sank into a chair.

"Maybe Hawkins is on his way out with Becky," Lauder said, patting his shoulder.

"Maybe," Rob agreed, "but he won't be taking her with him."

Elizabeth and Pauline had noticed the commotion and joined them.

"Have you heard something?" Pauline asked.

"Nothing good," Rob answered bitterly on his way out.

"Where are you going?" Elizabeth called after him.

"He's going after the child," Tully said. "It's a suicide mission. I wouldn't let him go if I were you."

Elizabeth let the weight of her remark sink in before she found Rob, feet planted, looking about him.

"Rob, don't do this," Elizabeth pleaded. "The captain says . . . ."

"Wait a minute," he interrupted.

"What?" Elizabeth asked.

"Where's Kane?"

CHAPTER TWENTY-EIGHT

A half mile along the mountain highway, Kane found the small dirt road that led into the forest. He had heard enough conversation about it to reason that this was the path that would deliver him to Becky. Earlier, after rushing practically unnoticed past the roadblock, he had passed a couple of pickup trucks occupied by firefighting personnel parked on the shoulder of the road. At one point he had to make way for a massive fire truck that was climbing the steep hill as it rushed to greet the fire at a point further up the highway.

Now, as the morning light filtered by smoke grew brighter, Kane launched himself onto the dirt road and raced toward the danger that he knew lay ahead. Danger, however, was not uppermost in his mind. His only thought was of the little girl.

Ashes fell from the sky like snowflakes, and falling embers occasionally ignited the brush, each small hot spot soon erupting into a full-fledged conflagration joining the massive flames that consumed the giant trees, closing in on the narrow road Kane had to navigate. Smoke filled his lungs, making it difficult to breathe.With each breath, he hoped for fresh air, but there was none to be had.

He had not been traveling long when he was stopped by the large black SUV driven by Hawkins. It loomed before him, encompassing the entire road, covering ground at a hazardous speed as he desperately sought to escape the fire which was closing in on both sides.

Kane was set to scramble out of the way when the vehicle suddenly skidded to a halt. Hawkins grabbed his wet towel and was about to race off on foot when he caught sight of the dog.

"You!" he growled.

Jumping back behind the wheel, he revved the engine and hit the gas, not bothering with the door.

Kane knew what he was up to the second he got behind the wheel, and he had plenty of time to get out of the way.

Hawkins cut the wheel sharply to hit him but smashed into a tree instead. Angrily shifting into reverse, he cut the wheel too fast and almost flipped over. The engine died.

"You son of a . . . . ." he grumbled.

It wouldn't start. The engine struggled to engage.

"Come on! Come on!" he yelled, frantically pumping the pedal, but it was hopeless.

Hawkins screamed like a wild thing, pounding on the dashboard with his fist until he finally hurt his hand. He was massaging, flexing his fingers when the sound of an approaching vehicle made him forget about the pain. He quickly grabbed his towel and put it over his mouth.

Within moments, the opposing vehicle came into view, and Kane's heart leaped as he recognized his friend Morris' beat-up blue Civic. There was a significant new dent in the hood and a few splinters of wood caught in the area where the windshield wipers lay.

Kane knew there was no time to spare. He checked the SUV, saw that Becky was not there, and rushed off.

Morris sat and allowed his engine to idle, taking in the situation. Hawkins recognized him and dropped the towel.

"Morris, you damn idiot!" he yelled. "Get outta the way!"

Morris made no attempt to move.

Yelling a profanity, Hawkins pulled the handgun stuffed in his belt and leaned out the window, firing off two shots in Morris' direction, putting two holes in the windshield, but missing the driver.

Morris placed his car into reverse and backed up several feet. Pausing for a moment, he shifted again and accelerated straight toward the SUV. Seeing he was about to be rammed, Hawkins hastily threw his gun onto the seat beside him and tried again to start his engine. He was just in time to swerve out of harm's way, but his left front wheel landed in a ditch. He could do nothing but scream as Morris plowed into him. The SUV was slammed into a burning tree, knocking a large branch loose. It came crashing down on the rear portion of the vehicle.

Miraculously, Morris' car was still running after the collision, and he backed it up several feet in case the burning tree should cause the other vehicle to explode. Jumping from his car and ignoring Hawkins' fate, he rushed in the direction Kane had headed but the dog was nowhere in sight and the fire had formed a wall behind him, making it impossible to follow.

Turning back to the SUV, Morris watched for a moment, wrestling with the urge to leave Hawkins to his fate before finally deciding to take action. Rushing toward the vehicle, he climbed up the side, the burning tree generating intense heat. Standing on the passenger's side, he used his foot to break the front passenger's window before leaning down and peering inside.

Squinting his eyes, Morris saw Hawkins laying against the driver's side door, barely conscious, his head severely injured. The handgun lay near his face, and it was with considerable effort that Morris was able to retrieve it.

"Hey," muttered Hawkins. "Help. Help me, man."

Disgusted, Morris hefted the weapon and considered his options. Hawkins was afraid he was going to kill him. His fear, like most of his emotions, turned to rage.

"Go on, you bastard!" he screamed. "Use it! You think I'm afraid to die?"

"I couldn't care less one way or the other," Morris told him. "You're just damn lucky I'm tryin' to do right by Jesus. They also gonna need you to testify against all them people you work with, so . . . give me your hand."

Hawkins meekly raised his hand toward Morris.

It was with considerable effort that the man was eventually freed from the burning vehicle in time before the flames from the burning tree finally ignited the gasoline and exploded. Before Morris transported his prisoner back down the road to turn him over to the police at the barricade, he paused for a moment to look off in the direction Kane was last seen.

"God bless you, buddy," he said. "I'll be waitin' for you."

Kane made his way through the inferno, whipped by the fierce wind, that would soon block the path ahead. The road was strewn with tree limbs and shrubbery which made the race he ran even more treacherous as he was forced to repeatedly alter course, zigzagging between objects, leaping over others. The pads on his feet were scorched, and he continually had to stop to shake burning embers from his long fur.

Along the road, Kane encountered a wooden bridge spanning a narrow stream of water that passed beneath on its journey to another point in the forest. As he crossed the bridge, his attention was briefly drawn to a number of animals, deer, rabbits, squirrels, skunks, and others, splashing their way through water increasingly filled with debris, as they followed its course in a desperate attempt to escape the flames. They took no note of him as they passed.

Kane was tempted to pause to take just a short drink to soothe his parched throat, but knowing that every second counted, he dared not delay. Clearing the bridge, he found conditions on the other side were no better.

He continued on, but it was hard to see and even harder to breathe. Soon his feet collapsed beneath him, and the collie lay on his side on the hot dirt road, panting heavily as he fought desperately for air.

Smoke filled his lungs, making him nauseous, and the pine needles made a hot, prickly bed. He fought to keep his eyes open. So long as he remained conscious, there was still a chance he would find Becky.

A wave of sadness swept over him. If only he were a little stronger, a little faster. If only he had followed his instincts in the first place, Becky would probably be in the kitchen right now, eating a cookie before anyone else was awake. It was their little secret.

Kane could feel himself slipping away when a shift in the wind revealed a sight too incredible to believe. He thought he was dreaming at first, but his eyes were open, and though it was little more than the silhouette of a rooftop amidst the smoke, he could see it was a cabin.

He dug his paws into the crunchy pine needles. His legs were weak and nothing had ever taxed him more, but gradually he found his strength and rose to his feet.

As he approached the small clearing that surrounded the cabin, his hopes were dashed when a thick, towering, Douglas-fir fell with a thunderous crash across his path, sending sparks in every direction. Flames leaped several feet into the air as thick plumes of fire exploded around him.

His fear was replaced by anger when he realized the tree blocked his path. He had never jumped as high as he would have to jump to clear the burning barricade and though his feeble strength might not be enough to support him, there was no time to think, only to act. The burning log was the only thing between him and Becky, and he would not be stopped.

Driving himself beyond the point of endurance, he gathered what little energy he had left and ran with all of his power toward the burning tree trunk. Reaching the barrier, he pushed himself upward with his hind legs and with all the force he could manage, lifted his body skyward, over the tree and through the vicious flames that singed his fur and burned his skin as he passed.

He barely managed to clear the hurdle, but his legs did not have the strength to hold him upright as he landed. His feet buckled, and he bounced and slid to a stop.

From where he lay he could see that the roof of the cabin was now ablaze, but he couldn't raise his head. He had to clear it first. A few seconds later he was back on his feet, racing to the cabin, managing the last few feet to reach the screen door of the porch. Pushing it with his paw, he bounced it open wide enough to pass through to the front door. Stopping there, he scratched on the closed door and barked loudly.

Becky's eyes went wide when she heard her friend and, pulling herself out of the traumatic spell in which she was drowning, she threw aside the blanket she had thrown over herself.

"Kane!" she screamed as she rushed to the door.

Opening the door, she grabbed her rescuer and pulled him across the threshold, kicking the door closed behind her. As he lay on the floor, nearly lifeless and panting, she wrapped her arms around him and held him close.

"I didn't think . . . . " she said to him. "Never mind. Let me get you some water!"

Rushing to the kitchen, she grabbed a bowl of artificial fruit from the table and emptied it on the floor. She used a chair to reach the faucet, but it was dry save a slight dribble of water. Quickly turning to the refrigerator, she found a plastic bottle of water and rushed back to Kane.

Dropping the bowl in front of him, she filled it with water, then threw the empty bottle aside and lifted Kane's head to help him drink.

"Please, Kane," she begged. "You need to drink!"

Her plea compelled him to lift his head slowly, and with substantial effort, he lapped at the cold liquid. Moving his tongue slowly at first, it felt good on his throat. Each swallow gave him strength, and with Becky's help and encouragement, he felt his senses renewed.

"Kane," Becky beseeched him, "You need to save me!"

As much as the water, her cry for help brought the dog back to life. Weary and weak, he stood and looked around the room.

There was a sudden, loud crack as a burning beam fell from the ceiling into the loft above them. Becky screamed and grabbed Kane.

Though he realized that the chance for survival was perhaps no better outside, for the moment, Kane knew he needed to get her out of the house before the roof caved in and he pulled away from her and scratched at the door. When Becky didn't move, he barked and scratched at the door again.

Becky opened the door and together they crossed the porch and opened the screen door leading outside.

Standing on the front porch steps, Kane surveyed the terrifying holocaust that surrounded them. Since he had been a young pup frisking about a mountain trail with the old man who had once been his constant friend, his favorite memories were of days amid the beautiful, green, fragrant, towering pines of the forest. It was a carefree feeling of freedom unlike any he had ever known, and his dreams were often filled with memories of the bliss and tranquility of the mountain woodlands. Kane had heard humans refer to a place called hell, but he had never fully understood its definition until now, and it was a place far worse than he could have imagined, far worse for having transformed what he had known as the most sacred place on earth into the catastrophe that now enveloped him.

"What can we do, Kane?" Becky screamed.

Circling repeatedly around the child he had hoped to save, Kane did all he could do to protect her from the flames. With every ounce of his strength and will he had managed to reach Becky, and now he grimly realized that there was no escape.

Though he had never contemplated death, it had occurred to him, abstractly, that someday he would again be reunited in the forest with the old man he had loved so dearly. But he doubted he would find his dear friend now. Not this way. Not in this forest.

"What can we do, Kane?" Becky screamed.

CHAPTER TWENTY-NINE

At dawn the next day, the beleaguered firefighters who had been risking their lives battling a forest fire of unimaginable strength were greeted with a combination of good news and bad. The winds had finally subsided, and although the fire was still less than twenty percent contained, the weather conditions promised a speedy defeat of the monster they had been fighting for two days.

The fire had moved quickly through and beyond the area surrounding Teller's cabin. Throughout the previous day and into the evening, Pauline, held tightly by her friend Elizabeth, refused to give up. Rob gave them updates, but there was little hope, and pretending otherwise was becoming more difficult.

An open cargo truck carrying a group of firefighters pulled into camp. They would have just enough time to catch their breath and grab a meal before they'd be back in harm's way. As the truck pulled to a stop, they dismounted and formed a line in front of Pauline, seated in a folding chair near the food truck. The men had found a patch of California poppies growing beside the road that had been untouched by the fire. It was late in the year for the wildflowers to be growing and even more unusual for them to be growing at that height, but there they stood, waving in the breeze. Each man who lined up before Pauline held in his hand a single poppy and each, in turn, handed a flower to her as they expressed condolences.

Pauline stared back at them blankly, lacking sleep, scarcely conscious of their presence.

A fire official stepped forward and placed a hand on Pauline's shoulder.

"Ma'am," he said to her, "we've set up a spare cot in the tent over here. Why don't you come and get some rest? We'll let you know if we hear anything."

"That's a good idea," Elizabeth joined in, placing an arm around Pauline's shoulder. "Come on, let's go."

In a zombie-like trance, Pauline allowed herself to be led away.

In the map tent, Rob, Lauder, and Captain Tully were looking at an at an aerial view of the cabin on her computer screen. Magnifying the image several times, she was able to provide them with a close-up view of the area where the cabin had once stood. All that remained was a concrete slab and a stone fireplace and chimney.

"Maybe she could have . . . . " Rob started, but his voice trailed off.

"She's a six-year-old child," Lauder said, touching his arm. "We questioned Hawkins before the boys took him away. He confessed to leaving her up there."

"She's still in there," Tully said, nodding at the screen.

"If there'd been any way to save her," came a voice from behind them, "Kane would've found it."

The trio turned to find Morris standing behind them. After turning Hawkins over to the police, he had remained, hoping to hear some news of Becky and Kane. Hawkins' confession that he had kidnapped the child and then left her to perish in the cabin was due in no small part to Morris' assistance.

A firefighter pulled up outside the tent in a jeep. Captain Tully left the group momentarily to exchange a few words with her subordinate, then returned.

"I've got a jeep and an ambulance," she announced to Rob and Lauder, "and we've got a dozer clearing the road to the cabin, so if you two gentlemen will follow me, we can get started now."

Rob told them he would join them momentarily and left to find Elizabeth in a tent nearby, sitting beside Pauline, who had finally succumbed to a deep slumber.

"We're going to take a look at the cabin," he quietly said to Elizabeth. "Will you be alright here for a while?"

She nodded.

"In case she wakes up," Elizabeth replied, suppressing a sob. "I don't want her to be alone if she does."

"Yeah," Rob said.

"And Rob," she added, "stop blaming yourself. For this, and for your brother."

Placing a hand on her shoulder, he leaned over and quietly placed a kiss on her forehead before heading for the jeep that was parked nearby.

When he arrived at the jeep, he found Captain Tully behind the steering wheel and Lauder sitting next to him. Morris was sitting in the back seat, a resolute expression on his face.

Rob paused before mounting he jeep.

"Maybe you ought to wait here," he said to him, but Morris emphatically shook his head.

"I'm goin' in there if I have to walk," he said with finality.

There was no argument to be won, so Rob climbed into the seat next to him. Captain Tully drove the jeep out of the camp, signaling the driver of an ambulance nearby to follow them.

After the short drive down the paved highway, the captain steered their vehicle onto the debris-strewn dirt road and slowly made her way along the pathway cleared by a bulldozer busy at work ahead of them. The acrid smell of smoke permeated the air. Amid the ashes, scattered embers still smoldered as the heavily dressed firefighters heaved buckets of water and shovel-fulls of dirt to extinguish them. Larger pockets of fire were being sprayed by men bearing hoses pumping water and foam from tanks mounted on the back of trucks dispersed throughout the grounds.

The remnants of the charred, blackened, trees stood gnarled and starkly naked against the smoldering ruins of the grey debris which was all that was left of the forest floor.

Along the way, they passed the demolished remains of Hawkins' SUV, still lying on its side, its skeletal frame nearly unrecognizable.

The wooden bridge that crossed the stream of water along the road no longer existed, but Captain Tully was able to maneuver the jeep through the water which, though polluted and littered, still managed to trickle its way across their path. The group paused on the opposite side of the stream to wait for the ambulance, which found the obstacle more challenging to cross.

No sign of life existed, and the landscape was littered with the charred remains of forest animals, burned beyond recognition. Though no one dared to say it, least of all Rob, nothing could have survived the apocalypse.

When they reached the point in their journey where the road led to the clearing around the cabin, they found the bulldozer struggling to remove the burned tree that had fallen across the path.

Rob waited impatiently for several minutes as the operator of the bulldozer arduously attempted to remove the barrier. When it had been pushed far enough to one side for a person to clear it, Rob started to move.

"Don't even think about it," Tully said to him.

"I can't just sit here," Rob replied, jumping from the jeep.

Turning sideways, he was able to make his way past the barrier, his clothes brushing against the warm trunk. Seeing his success, the others followed.

Rob stood in the clearing that surrounded the cabin area, aghast at the sight before him. The aerial view he had seen on the computer screen didn't prepare him for the deadly devastation he now beheld.

The blackened stone fireplace and chimney stood tall amid the black ashes. Rob could barely recognize a few pieces made of steel and metal that had not wholly perished in the inferno. There were remnants of a refrigerator, a twisted bit that may have once been the base of a chandelier, and other objects destroyed beyond recognition. The ugliness of the sight and what it told him about anyone who might have been left inside turned his legs to mush, and he fell to his knees in despair.

Lauder patted him on the back. The rest stood in silence. The bulldozer had finally managed to clear a passageway for the ambulance, which now drove around them and parked in front of the cabin's remnants. The two paramedics exited the vehicle and surveyed the damage.

Having completed his job, the bulldozer operator cut his engine. What followed was an eerie silence. No birds were chirping above, there was no breeze blowing through the branches of the trees and no leaves or greenery to stir, and the group said nothing as they stood reverently contemplating the deadly panorama spread before them.

It was in that silence that a sound, faint and unrecognizable at first, began to intensify. Captain Tully and the men exchanged glances, the expression on their faces asking one another, "Do you hear that?"

"Over there!" one of the paramedics called out, pointing off in the distance.

"Listen!" Rob ordered, commanding silence. After a moment he was certain, and he finally identified the sound to be the bark of a dog, echoing through the mountains.

Elated, he yelled, "Kane!"

Rob rose to his feet, slightly stumbling as he did so and began running toward the source of the sound, and the others followed. The paramedics grabbed a stretcher and trailed in their wake.

Occasionally pausing briefly to identify the direction from which the sound emanated and after a couple of wrong turns, Rob frequently stumbling in his eagerness, was able to make his way through the rubble and fragments the fire left behind. When the barking stopped, Rob paused, breathing heavily.

"Kane!" he shouted.

The barking resumed. Closer this time.

"It *is* him!" he yelled excitedly to the others, and he began running again without waiting for them.

They found Kane, barely standing, barely recognizable beneath soot, black mud and singed fur. He held up an injured front paw. Behind him ran the stream that passed in that direction on its way to the damaged bridge they had crossed.

Rob rushed to the dog and knelt to embrace him, but as he did so, Kane pulled away. He stood for a moment, locked eyes with Rob, then turned and hobbled toward the water, with Lauder at his heels.

At this point, the stream widened and fell in a rush over a steep rock, creating a small waterfall as it cascaded into a pool, about three feet deep. Kane stepped into the stream and began barking at the falling water.

Rob peered into the area Kane was indicating. It wasn't until he saw something moving behind the waterfall, a seemingly shapeless shadow, that he understood.

"My God!" he exclaimed with a grin. "The back side of water!"

"What the hell are you talking about?" Lauder asked.

Rob didn't answer. He splashed through the water as Kane continued to bark. Reaching into the area behind the falling water, he found what he was looking for, and he lifted Becky into his arms. She was shaking and only half conscious.

"Is Kane alright?" she asked faintly.

"He's fine, honey," Rob said with a laugh.

She nodded and passed out.

He carried her across the water and laid her on the dry ground as the paramedics arrived on the scene. They quickly checked her vitals.

"She's unconscious. Let's get her to the hospital," one of them said, and they moved her onto the stretcher and prepared to lift her.

"Wait!" Rob said.

Kane, who had been watching close nearby, now moved in and lay next to her. Whining softly, he looked into her face and began licking her cheek tenderly. Within moments, the little girl stirred and coughed before opening her eyes as if from a deep sleep. At first, squinting at the people leaning over her, she turned her head and saw the face of the collie who lay next to her.

"Kane!" she said with a smile and threw her arms around him.

"Kane," she repeated with satisfaction and closed her eyes.

"Let's move," one of the paramedics said.

Kane didn't want to leave her and Rob had to pull him away as the two men lifted the stretcher. As they rushed away, the collie tried to follow after them, but with his injuries he could barely move.

Rob pulled his phone from his pocket and looked at the screen.

"Yes!" he exclaimed when he saw that he was able to get reception.

Turning to Lauder and Tully, he asked, "Mind if I tell Pauline?"

Lauder smiled and Rob began dialing as they followed the paramedics.

Kane was hobbling behind, but all of the strength he had brought to bear in his rescue of Becky was completely used up.

Finally, and with nothing left to keep him going, he collapsed. Becky was safe, he thought. It was all right. He could rest now.

It was then that a hand reached out to him and touched his head. Kane thought it must have been the hand of the old man he had revered so dearly for all those years before he came to live with Ben, and with that thought, he drifted into deep sleep, thoroughly used up and exhausted but feeling the affection in that touch that told him he was loved.

Morris had lingered behind the others to watch after Kane. He continued to stroke the dog's singed fur until he was sure Kane was asleep, which wasn't long. Then, gently lifting him, Morris carried Kane from the ruins of the forest.

CHAPTER THIRTY

The unholy alliance between the mayor and the drug gangs of Los Angeles hit the news, and within a week, federal agents swarmed city hall and placed Mayor Robbins and Executive Assistant to the Mayor Richard Teller under arrest. It was national news.

Typically, trials were delayed for a couple of years. The evidence against them was so extensive, however, and the individuals connected to the crime so numerous, there was no call for the defense to ask for extensions, for a change. Several teams of prosecutors quickly assembled their case. In the end, the mayor received a prison sentence much lighter than he deserved due to his insistence that he was merely Richard Teller's puppet and had little knowledge of the day to day operations of the program. Since Teller did indeed plan and execute the entire enterprise himself, the executive assistant's lawyers could offer very little in his defense, particularly after Rodney Hawkins struck a deal with prosecutors: life without parole. Teller got 99 years.

Once Captain Takimoto began looking into Officer Glasser's finances, and his ability to afford the new Lexus he was driving, it was a very short thread that led to the other dirty cops who were part of Teller's team. The worst punishment Glasser received was the loss of his job and the Lexus. Many of the other suspects didn't get off as lightly.

Captain Takimoto also managed to persuade his superiors to erase Zach Burton's negative record with his department, making his widow and daughter eligible to receive his police pension.

Detective Mosher finally received the promotion he had sought for so long, and one of his first duties as lieutenant was to bring Officer Rob Martinez onto his unit. As homicide detectives, Rob and his old friend Danny Ralston made a formidable team.

Elizabeth returned to UC Davis School of Veterinary Medicine and resumed her studies in earnest. She still found time for Police Detective Martinez, who frequently dropped by her school for a visit. As time allowed, she reciprocated by visiting him in Los Angeles, and on holidays they often met at her parents' home. Elizabeth had made no commitment to him, but Rob was willing to wait. Danny told his partner he was a dreamer.

"Maybe," Rob mused, "but dreams do come true, and she's worth the wait."

Rob and James Morris had another meeting one evening at the same bench in front of the entrance to the Los Angeles Zoo. His shabby little blue Civic was nowhere to be seen in the parking lot. It hadn't been the same after its encounter with the Lincoln Navigator, and Morris had to resign himself to putting it to rest.

"I never thanked you for all you did," Rob said, "for Zach, for me, for Kane and Becky, hell, for the whole damn city of Los Angeles. We're in your debt. You know that?"

"That what you come up here to tell me, man?" Morris asked with a frown. "Hell, if I did it for anybody I prob'ly did it for myself. Ain't that why we all do things? We claim it's for somebody else, but maybe we just do it to make ourselves feel better."

"You think Kane did everything he did to make himself feel better?" Rob countered. "I'd say dogs spend their whole lives trying to make other people feel better. And they never even expect any thanks."

"Yeah, well, Kane's different. You know that. Ain't no people like Kane. How's my friend doin', anyhow?"

"He's doing fine. He'll be heading back home soon, him and Elizabeth."

Morris nodded and smiled.

"Good," he said. "Well, Detective, if you ain't got no further business with me I'll be goin' now."

"Hold on there," Rob said. "Where are you going? What are you going to be doing with your life?"

"Hell, I don't know," Morris answered, gesturing toward the city with a wave. "Just keep on doin' what I been doin' I guess, 'til Hawkins puts out the hit on me."

"You don't have to go back to that life," Rob insisted, "Let me help you find a job that . . . ."

"Naw," Morris interrupted. "I'll disappear somewhere. Try to hide out. Maybe find me a puppy. Think ol' Kane would like me to do that?"

"I think that would make Kane very happy," Rob said with a chuckle.

"Alright then," Morris replied with a nod. "You give him a hug for me when you see him next time. Take care, now. Maybe I'll see you around."

Rob watched Morris walk away until he disappeared from view. It was the last time he ever saw him.

On a crisp, bright, spring day following the summer the winds swept hell through the mountains near Big Bear Lake, Pauline and Becky accepted May's invitation to visit her family at their vineyard in the hills above Santa Barbara. Elizabeth was home from school for spring break, and Rob was expected to drop by later.

May helped Pauline unload her suitcase and escorted her into the house. She explained that her husband, Paul, was working the fields, having recently returned from Afghanistan. He had accepted a partnership with the company that had leased their property during his absence,and he was home to stay and would now, he vowed, dedicate the rest of his life rebuilding his relationship with his family and, in particular, with his son.

The religious moment that had possessed May when she sensed that Ben would survive his battle with cancer proved to be prescient. After extensive tests, his doctors declared him cancer-free, though they tempered the good news with caution. Such cases as Ben's were notorious for their instance of re-occurrence. Today, however, she refused to entertain any such possibility, and she managed to balance her time between teaching school, volunteering at church and working to educate the public about the poor financial support childhood cancer received from the government. It was an issue about which she had become passionate.

Becky rushed up the stairs ahead of her mother and into the house.

"Kane!" she called out. "Kane! Where are you?"

"That dog is all she's been able to talk about since last summer," Pauline said.

"Well," May said with a smile, "I think she has good reason, don't you think?"

Hearing Becky's voice, Elizabeth rushed down the stairs from her bedroom and gleefully greeted her.

Becky politely returned Elizabeth's hug but continued to look around the house.

"Excuse me, " she said. "Where's Kane?"

Taking Pauline's hand, she led her onto the porch outside the back door, followed by Pauline and May. For a moment Elizabeth stood, her hand blocking the sun as she surveyed the fields for a sign of the collie.

Looking across the rolling hills, she spotted Ben, a stick in his hand as he marched up and down the vineyards.

"Ah!" Elizabeth said as she leaned down to Becky and pointed him out. "There's Ben. Kane won't be too far away from him. Go ask him."

Without a word, Becky rushed down the stairs and into the field.

She had been adjusting well since the events of the preceding year, thanks to psychological assistance she had been receiving, Pauline told them, and she had made several new friends at school. She surprised her teachers with her advanced reading level. Dog books remained her favorite.

No one ever knew for sure whose idea it was to seek protection behind the back side of water during the fire. Becky didn't like to talk about that day, and so it remained a secret between her and Kane.

"Hi, Ben," she said as she eagerly rushed up to him. "Where's Kane?"

Ben was deep in thought, but he finally returned her greeting with a simple, unemotional, "Hi."

Looking around, he pointed with his stick to a nearby hill, atop which there rested a tall, old, oak tree.

"Oh," he said, "Kane's probably up there. That's his favorite spot."

Wasting no time thanking him, Becky ran toward the hill, startling several cottontails which fled for cover as she whizzed by.

Kane was dozing, his feet twitching as he dreamed a dream that he was a puppy again, barking as he ran through a vast field of grass and poppies with his littermates, joyful and carefree. In his deep slumber he was unaware of Becky's approach, and as she drew near, she slowed down to a walk. Cautiously and quietly, so as not to wake him, she sat next to him and slowly stroked his fur.

So softly did she touch him, and so immersed in his dream was he, that he was at first unaware of her presence until, finally, he slowly opened his eyes. Turning his head, he looked up into the little girl's face, and when he recognized her, he languidly wagged his tail and laid his head in her lap. Shifting his body slightly for comfort, he exhaled with sublime contentment, long and blissful, before drifting back to sleep.

Grateful acknowledgment is made to the following organizations for the work they perform on behalf of children everywhere:

Children's Cancer Therapy Development Institute

12655 SW Beaverdam Rd.

West Beaverton, OR 97005

info@cc-tdi.org

The Children's Advocacy Center for Child Abuse Assessment and Treatment

1650 E. Old Badillo St. #C3

Covina, CA. 91724

http://childrensadvocacyctr.org/

Pet Prescription Team Pet Therapy Organization

1920 Dehesa Rd

El Cajon, CA 92019

http://www.petprescriptionteam.com

www.ingramcontent.com/pod-product-compliance
Lightning Source LLC
Chambersburg PA
CBHW071605110726
47908CB00007B/2250